A Forgotten Fall

A Lord For All Seasons
Book 3

Nadine Millard

© Copyright 2022 by Nadine Millard
Text by Nadine Millard
Cover by Dar Albert

Dragonblade Publishing, Inc. is an imprint of Kathryn Le Veque Novels, Inc.
P.O. Box 23
Moreno Valley, CA 92556
ceo@dragonbladepublishing.com

Produced in the United States of America

First Edition September 2022
Trade Paperback Edition

Reproduction of any kind except where it pertains to short quotes in relation to advertising or promotion is strictly prohibited.

All Rights Reserved.

The characters and events portrayed in this book are fictitious. Any similarity to real persons, living or dead, is purely coincidental and not intended by the author.

ARE YOU SIGNED UP FOR DRAGONBLADE'S BLOG?

You'll get the latest news and information on exclusive giveaways, exclusive excerpts, coming releases, sales, free books, cover reveals and more.

Check out our complete list of authors, too!

No spam, no junk. That's a promise!

Sign Up Here

www.dragonbladepublishing.com

Dearest Reader;

Thank you for your support of a small press. At Dragonblade Publishing, we strive to bring you the highest quality Historical Romance from some of the best authors in the business. Without your support, there is no 'us', so we sincerely hope you adore these stories and find some new favorite authors along the way.

Happy Reading!

CEO, Dragonblade Publishing

Additional Dragonblade books by
Author Nadine Millard

A Lord For All Seasons Series
A Springtime Scandal (Book 1)
Midsummer Madness (Book 2)
A Forgotten Fall (Book 3)

Prologue

"Look, Hope. There's Adam Fairchild. Do you think he'll ask you to dance tomorrow night?"

Francesca Templeworth ignored the odd flip her stomach did as she listened to her older sisters discuss the party they were to attend at the Marquess of Heywood's country home tomorrow. It was all everyone in Halton could talk about. The marquess sometimes spent Christmastide at the rambling old manse with his two sons, Douglas and Adam. This year, they had arrived just as the leaves were turning red and gold at the start of autumn. The elder was as stoic and unforgiving as his father. But Adam Fairchild had always been easy-going and charming.

Even talk about the war, which had everyone else up in the boughs, didn't seem to dim his smile or the wicked glint in his moss-green eyes. But it was making everyone nervous. Everyone except Mama, who kept referring to it as "that ghastly French business"; Hope, who went into a fit of raptures every time she saw a red coat and was a fan of any occasion that caused an abundance of them to be seen in Halton; and Sophia, who was too young to care.

But Cheska wasn't too young to care. And she cared. A lot. She cared that the young men and boys she'd grown up with were dying. Or returning with missing limbs. Sometimes missing sanity, it seemed. And she cared that, as a girl, there was nothing she could do to help their cause.

She *could* help. Had the ability to help. She just wasn't allowed to.

"Cheska? Are you even listening?"

Cheska blinked at Sophia's demanding tone. The youngest, and only two years Francesca's junior, Sophia was already stubborn enough to give all the Templeworth girls a little competition in that area. Except for Elodie, of course, who was a paragon of virtue.

"No," Cheska answered, flicking a bright golden lock over her shoulder. "I'm not."

She would never in a million years admit that the talk of Hope, who was undeniably stunning, flirting with Adam Fairchild made her feel vaguely ill. It wasn't that she was interested in Adam in any case. He was too old, for a start. Six years her senior. A man, whilst she was still a girl. But—well, he was one of the very few people in Halton who listened to Cheska talk about the things that interested her without his eyes glazing over with boredom. Or without frowning in disapproval as the ladies of their tiny town did. Or without being disgusted at a young lady not only daring to be knowledgeable about such things but actually audacious enough to be vocal about them. Or worst of all, pretend to listen for a moment or two, then interrupt her to ask about Hope.

Adam Fairchild shared her views about the war. Shared her views about politics. Had even read some of Mary Wollstonecraft's writings, claiming that he felt obliged to since Francesca had already done so at such an early age.

"Well, you should be," Sophia snapped back, interrupting Francesca's rambling thoughts. "What if I'm saying something terribly important?"

"If it's about yet another man's tongue wagging over Hope, I don't think that constitutes terribly important."

"It does to me," Hope piped up, her deep, brown eyes sparkling with mischief. "Especially if it's a tongue as delectable as Adam Fairchild's."

"Hope, really," Elodie interrupted. "Must you speak in such a fashion, especially in public?"

"Yes," Hope answered. "And if you scold me, I'll say it louder."

Cheska grinned at Elodie's panicked expression, at her sister's brown eyes the same shade as Hope's, widening in terror.

"Regardless of how delectable his tongue may or may not be, I wouldn't get too close, Hope. It won't be long before he's off to war." Francesca ignored that odd feeling in her belly as she spoke the words. She knew Adam intended to go to war because he'd told her so just the other day when she'd been lamenting the fact that she couldn't do the same thing.

"Well then perhaps I'll give him a going away present to remember," Hope said, laughing herself silly at Elodie's gasp of outrage. And in the end, Adam didn't get the chance to even say hello to Hope, because Elodie dragged them all home.

CHESKA WATCHED FROM the doors to the balcony as Adam did indeed dance with Hope. They made a striking pair, she had to admit to herself. Like two golden gods dancing together. Though Adam's hair was more sandy-brown than gold, and his eyes were that captivating green.

Francesca hadn't danced. She was only there because Adam insisted she attend his farewell ball. Rather alarmingly, she'd been approached by more than one lecherous old oaf and was now engaged in sending daggers to any young man foolish enough to approach her.

The reel she was watching from the doorway came to a halt, and Cheska took the opportunity to slip outside. Some time alone. That would set her to rights. That would calm this odd, aching *thing* in the pit of her stomach.

She breathed a deep sigh, inhaling the sharpness of the cool evening and relishing the time alone.

"You are quite the escape artist. Nobody even saw you leave."

Francesca turned up to see Adam grinning down at her, his smile doing enough funny things to her insides that she panicked and plastered a look of boredom on her face.

"Except you, apparently," she drawled.

Her bad mood didn't seem to affect his jovial one in the slightest if his laugh was any indication. "Ah, well. A good soldier knows to keep an eye on the goings on around him," he quipped, coming to stand beside her at the balustrade against which she leaned. They both gazed out over the impressive, darkened gardens of Heywood Manor, his father's home here in Halton. A beautiful, perfectly kept structure.

Francesca's stomach once again tightened painfully. Just this evening, the marquess had announced that both his sons were leaving to fight. The gathered crowd had been stunned. Francesca included. Though she'd known of Adam's plans, his brother Douglas, the heir to the marquisette—that was a shock to everyone. They'd all assumed Lord Heywood would keep his eldest at home so that he could safely ensure the continuation of the line, as many titled families were doing.

"I'm surprised at your father agreeing to you and your brother going," she said carefully. She knew that Lord Heywood was a lot less concerned about his spare than his heir. And she knew because Adam had told her so in that irreverent, devil-may-care way. But it seemed cruel to just comment on his brother's enlisting.

The quirk of his lips, however, told Francesca that he knew what she was doing.

"Nobody can tell Douglas what he can or cannot do," he responded calmly. "Not even the mighty Marquess of Heywood. But he wasn't best pleased if that's what you're wondering."

Cheska felt a stab of irritation at his words. Usually, nobody could tell her what to do either. But short of stowing away on a ship, she'd be left here to paint and sew and engage in all manner of mind-numbing, vacuous pursuits, being seen as nothing but a broodmare for whatever gentleman offered the most advantages.

And what she was feeling must have shown on her face, for Adam reached out and tweaked a golden tendril that had come loose from her pinned curls.

"Don't wish for it, Sunshine," he warned her, laughing at her scowl. "It won't be the adventure you might think it." She must have told him a hundred times that the nickname he'd given her made her feel silly and girlish. He'd told her it was her own fault for having hair as bright as the sun and then laughed as she'd pretended to cast up her accounts at the flowery words.

"I don't think it will be anything other than harrowing and devastating," she said as she batted his hand away. "I just hate that I can't *do* anything. That I can't help. In any capacity. That I'll be stuck here until I'm handed off to some gentleman like a prize for having enough money and social standing to satisfy Mama."

He studied her for an age, those eyes gazing into her own.

"You will find a way to help, Sunshine," he said, his words so imbued with sincerity that she didn't even scold him for the moniker. "If anyone can find her own path to carve, it's you."

Francesca was suddenly overwhelmed with sadness. Sadness that he was leaving. And that she had no idea if or when she'd see him again.

"And what of your own path?" she dared to ask. "Will it lead you back here?"

He reached out and squeezed her hand. A friendly, platonic gesture she was sure, but one that set her heart alight.

"Perhaps," was all he said. "One day."

Chapter One

Eight Years Later...

"Georgie, Ollie, you can't leave out Ella and Lily. You must play nicely."

Cheska had to shout to be heard over the squalling of her youngest niece and the latest arrival to their family. Little Helena, or Nell as they'd already taken to calling her, was only months old, but she could cry loud enough to bring down a mountain. Which was what she was currently doing.

Gideon, ever the doting papa, was doing his best to console the little tigress, but until Hope came to feed her, there would be no peace, and they all knew it. Oliver and Lily had been the same. George and Ella had been slightly less vocal in their demands as babes, seeming to have inherited Elodie's more placid temperament. Though now, at ages six and three, respectively, they were developing some of that Templeworth temper, as Christian had dubbed it.

Francesca winced at a particularly loud squall and wondered not for the first time why both her sisters had chosen to shirk the usual wetnurse in favor of nursing their own children. It would certainly be a lot quieter.

"But they're girls, Aunt Cheska. They can't do it."

Francesca opened her mouth to answer George, but before she got a chance to, his father laughed and interrupted.

"You've picked the wrong lady to make that particular argument to, son." Christian grinned. "Your aunt will no doubt tell you that the girls are perfectly capable of catching fish. And she would be right," he continued, his voice growing sterner as the stubborn young lord looked set to argue.

Francesca's heart melted at the pout on George's lips. He was adorable with his mop of dark curls like his father and big brown eyes like his mama. All the children were adorable as a matter of fact, and Cheska had no idea how their parents ever managed to scold them when they looked at them so.

She watched, her lips twitching with amusement as Christian and George engaged in a standoff, wondering who would win. She would wager that it would be Christian. Because whilst George could sulk as well as his father, he was an easygoing little soul. If it had been Ella standing there arguing, Francesca knew Christian would have been the first to break.

Hope hurried into the garden and plucked Nell out of Gideon's arms before darting back inside with the babe with a quick grin in Christian's direction.

Finally, the little boy gave in.

"Fine," he said in a tone that let the entire garden know he was none-too-pleased about it. "They can come, but you must tell her father that she can't keep fishing for mermaids. It's silly."

Francesca eyed her nephew, wondering if he had already stopped believing in the myths and magic of his bedtime stories. But then he continued.

"As though they'd be able to get from the ocean to a lake."

The adults shared a conspiratorial smile at the mix of innocence and condescension, and Francesca watched as Gideon and Christian rounded up the children and brought them all, still bickering, to the lake on the boundary of her father's grounds.

The silence fell around her in the chill, autumn air, and she heaved a sigh torn between being grateful for the sudden peace and an odd, aching feeling that, if she didn't know any better, she'd call loneliness.

She was never lonely. Never allowed herself to feel something so nonsensical. Her older sisters were happy with husbands who adored them. Sophia was happy as long as she was surrounded by horses and hay. And Francesca was happy when she was left alone to read and think and not have to make inane chitchat with vacuous ladies or listen to odious men while they sweated and slobbered over her.

It was just odd. Odd that her sisters had moved away, only home now because Papa had fallen ill, and Mama was using it as an excuse to get her sons-in-law back to Halton to show them off. She never tired of ensuring that everyone knew she had a viscount and an earl in the family. And even though Cheska had insisted that she was more than capable of running things whilst Papa recovered, her mother was never going to pass up the opportunity to get Christian and Gideon here.

It was infuriating, but Cheska had learned that her mother was a militant social climber, and nothing would change that. Papa could have had a trifling cold, and she'd have dragged Christian and Gideon to Halton for it.

But irritating as it was to be treated as though she couldn't run the household and estate for a couple of weeks until Papa felt better, it *was* nice to have them here. Not just Elle and Hope, but their husbands and children, too. Christian and Gideon might be a little watchful, overprotective even, but she was fond enough of them that she let a lot of it go in favor of keeping the peace.

"There you are. Why are you hiding in the garden?"

Francesca turned at the sound of Sophia's voice to see her younger sister striding across the lawn toward her, clad in her usual breeches with her chestnut hair flying down her back.

"I'm not hiding." Cheska rolled her eyes. "Christian and Gideon have just gone to the lake. Why did you think I was hiding anyway?"

Sophia sighed as she dropped to the bench beside Cheska. "Mrs. Carstairs is here," she said.

"Damn and blast," Cheska spat, free to swear to her heart's

content with Elodie out of earshot. "What trouble is the old bat stirring up now?"

Mrs. Carstairs had always been a spiteful gossip, gleefully spreading rumors and tearing people's lives apart for years. Unfortunately, she was also one of Mama's closest cronies and made no secret of the fact that she spied relentlessly on the Templeworth girls in the hopes that she could spread a truly ruinous scandal about them. It baffled Cheska that Mama considered the spiteful woman a friend. But then, truth be told, Mama was no better when it came to scandal and gossip. Thankfully, she'd never found out about Elodie and Christian's less-than-perfect start given that Christian had accidentally kidnapped Elle and taken her to London.

And Hope swimming practically naked when she'd met Gideon for the first time had somehow remained a secret.

Though the entirety of Halton knew that Cheska and her sisters weren't exactly sticklers for the rules of polite society, they'd never done anything truly irreparable. Well, they hadn't been *caught* doing anything irreparable. Though there was still time, she supposed.

Sophia scowled toward the house, oblivious to Francesca's inner thoughts. "This time it's not actually about us," she said. "Not yet in any case. I'm sure that given enough time she'll come up with something."

"Mm. More than likely about me."

"Oh, yes. She *despises* you," Sophia said cheerfully. "And now that she fawns over Hope and her title as countess, you're quite on your own."

"Yes, I did notice that you've had it rather easy with the old goat's censure. How on earth have you managed it?"

"She's probably still hoping I'll marry that vile son of hers." Sophia shuddered, and Francesca winced in sympathy. It was no secret that Hubert Carstairs had been sniffing around Sophia for years now. After he'd been rejected by Hope and rejected *and* slapped by Francesca. Sophia was his last chance to have one of them. Something he'd felt it appropriate to tell her the last time he'd called.

"Anyway, I left the drawing room before she'd even been announced. As soon as I saw her carriage, in fact. All I heard on the way out was the Marquess of Heywood."

Francesca's entire body tensed as a maelstrom of emotions hit her at Sophia's words.

The Marquess of Heywood.

Nobody in Halton had so much as whispered the title since the tragedy years ago. Since Douglas Fairchild had been killed in battle, and Adam—here her heart squeezed painfully, even after all this time—Adam had gone missing and was now presumed dead. The marquess hadn't recovered from such a terrible, awful loss and had died only a year later, leaving the Halton house to fall into disuse, and the locals to wonder about who the new marquess might be.

After a time, everyone had stopped talking about it, stopped wondering. But Francesca never did. Just as she had never been able to stop the foolish hope that Adam was still alive somewhere.

"What did she say about him? The new marquess. Have they tracked down that cousin of Lord Heywood?" she demanded, remembering that there'd been talk of a long-distance relative that might make a claim to the marquessate.

Sophia's eyes widened, most likely surprised by the urgency in Francesca's tone that she couldn't quite control.

"How should I know?" Sophia asked. "Didn't I just tell you I had the sense to run when I saw her coming? But if there *is* finally a newly found marquess, he must be in Halton. Or at least coming to it. Mrs. Carstairs is far too interested in local gossip to bother looking further afield."

Francesca barely managed a mumble of agreement, her mind racing with memories and grief and dizzying thoughts. And before she quite knew what she was about, she was on her feet and gazing over the hedgerows bordering the formal gardens as though she could see Heywood Manor from here.

"What are you…"

"I'm going for a walk," Cheska blurted, interrupting whatever Sophia was about to say.

"Oh. Well, I can join you if—"

"No, that's quite all right. You have your horses to see to. I'll see you later."

Feeling Sophia's eyes on her back, Francesca hurried toward the laneway that would cut past the village and toward Heywood Manor, questioning her sanity the entire way.

Chapter Two

"THAT'S THE LAST of it, my lord."

Adam Fairchild turned, flinching internally at the title that still sat awkwardly on his shoulders after all this time.

Coming back to Halton was supposed to bring him some measure of peace, however small. Give him a refuge from every nightmare, every second of mental torture he'd endured for the last eight years.

But hearing the servants address him as Lord Heywood was still as harrowing as it had been in France. And again, in Belgium. And in London. He shouldn't be Lord Heywood. This was never supposed to be his life. There might be a lot of things he couldn't remember since his accident, but he remembered that in excruciating detail. Remembered the injury that had almost killed him. Remembered receiving the news that Douglas had been killed in battle only miles from where he himself had almost been killed. And remembered the letter that told him of his father's demise and his own catapult from last heir standing to the marquess.

Some days, when the pain in his head grew worse than the pain in his soul, his thoughts and memories became fuzzy and unreliable. Other days, waking nightmares plagued him so much that he couldn't seem to tell the present from the past. But through it all was the gaping hole where his family had once been. A gap that would never be filled and could never be forgotten. A dark absence where his brother and father should be.

Coming to Halton had been a mistake. A foolish decision taken in the dark at the bottom of a brandy bottle. The French might have been bastards in the war, but at least they could produce a decent drink. Still, that same drink was largely responsible for this mess. Him standing in the middle of the courtyard that the house's loyal, skeleton staff had kept in good repair, even while he'd been missing. And they hadn't known where the coin for their services would come from.

One of the first things he'd done on his return to London had been to ensure that the sizeable staff at all his holdings were paid and rewarded handsomely. It had been a strange year. From the moment he'd set foot back on English soil, he'd gone through the motions of being the marquess insofar as running the estates and business interests went.

He'd avoided parliament, lest he be expected to function properly as anything other than a shell of the man he once was. He'd happily handed over most of his responsibilities to stewards and solicitors, and then he'd hidden away, content to drown every dark thought, every unbearable wave of grief, every painful memory, and horrible episode of confusion and panic in bottle after bottle.

Finally, when he'd almost drunk his cellars dry, he'd received a visit from an old friend intent on stopping him from drinking himself into an early grave. Devon Blake, Duke of Farnshire, had been a childhood friend with whom Adam kept up a correspondence. Face-to-face meetings were rare, since Farnshire's seat was in the wilds of Scotland. But as it happened, Devon had been in Town and had heard the never-ending chatter about Adam teetering on the brink of insanity.

"*Come to Farnshire,*" Devon had tried to coax him. "*The city isn't doing you any good.*"

Of course, the city wasn't doing him any good. Nowhere was doing him any good. But Farnshire, isolated and beautiful as it was, wouldn't help. Devon wasn't the fussing sort, but nor would he allow Adam to slip into oblivion from morning to night. And that's all he wanted these days. On the days that the memories were so bad, they kept him abed, panic and grief and guilt slammed into him in a never-ending maelstrom.

But Devon's suggestion had sparked something in Adam, and he'd found himself feeling even more miserable in Town. Of course, he never ventured out. Especially during the Season, where he knew hundreds if not thousands of eyes would be upon him. Hundreds of tongues would be wagging with their vicious gossip or even worse, empty sympathy. And most of all, desperate mamas trying to push him into marriage with their equally desperate daughters.

Nobody would care that he was broken. Nobody would care that he'd completely forgotten the man he'd been before. All they'd see was an old, lauded title and the wealth that came with it. A title and wealth that had separated him from the men he'd ended up bleeding with. The men who'd fought to keep his brother alive, even if they'd ultimately failed.

It was when the first callers braved his front door, an old friend of his father's and his beady-eyed daughter, that the spark Devon had ignited grew to a flame. Like hell would he stay here and be fawned over like he'd achieved something by being the last man standing in his family. But where could he go that wouldn't feel like another cage? Where could he go to feel even a modicum of peace, however fleeting?

And then, suddenly, he'd remembered Halton. That odd little town that had given him so much happiness in his youth. The oddities that made up the townsfolk. That family of wild, bold, and brazen girls, whose names escaped him now. His memory wasn't what it used to be since he'd been shot from his horse in battle. But he'd remembered Heywood Manor with perfect clarity. And how happy he'd been there.

It had taken him only days to make arrangements to travel here since he didn't exactly have a rake of people to bid farewell to, and he'd kept a small staff at Heywood just like his other properties. And so it was that he found himself standing here being battered by memories of the past. Feeling as though the weight of his responsibilities, ones he'd never wanted in the first place, could bring him to his knees.

Suddenly coming here seemed like the stupidest of ideas. Adam had no idea why he'd thought his life would be more bearable in Halton.

He had half a mind to just tell the servants to pack everything up again. He'd only brought a valet. And that was because the old codger refused to leave his side. Simmons had been his father's valet. And should have been Douglas's. Not Adam's. But sometimes the stubborn old man was the only thing standing in the way of Adam completely losing his tenuous grip on sanity, and he'd come to rely on that more than he would have thought possible.

He hated how weak it made him, this lack of control over his emotions. Sometimes he felt as though he'd give his very soul to escape his own head. This had been a bad idea.

"So, it's true. You're back."

The sound of a female voice, husky and demanding, broke through Adam's tumultuous thoughts, and he whipped around toward it.

Standing before him was a beautiful, golden-haired woman with the widest, bluest eyes he'd ever seen. He couldn't quite stop his gaze from running over her incredulously. Not much had held his interest for long after the last few years, but whoever this was, she was definitely holding it.

The cut of her simple blue gown was elegant enough to tell him that she was likely Quality, as was the regal tilt of her chin. But the loose tumble of curls and the fact that she'd arrived here unannounced and unaccompanied, told him that Quality or not, she certainly didn't seem the usual, gently bred type.

Something was nagging in the back of his mind. Some hazy memory becoming clear as she frowned up at him, her eyes sparkling in the autumn sun.

"Adam?"

Suddenly, he remembered. To his shock, he remembered her with perfect clarity. And for the first time in years, he managed a smile.

"Hello, Sunshine."

Chapter Three

FRANCESCA'S HEART FLUTTERED wildly in her chest at the sound of Adam Fairchild's deep baritone. It was him. It was really him. And yet, not.

Her eyes ran over him of their own accord, drinking in every inch of him. From the towering height and broad shoulders to the tiny scar at his temple. Time had brought about great changes in him. He was bigger. Older. Darker.

But it was his eyes that shocked her the most. The striking green which had always been so full of mischief, so full of life and joy, were now dull and empty. Hollow, even. And it made her feel surprisingly sorrowful.

She'd practically run all the way over here just to see if it was true. If he'd somehow miraculously returned from the dead. Of course, he *hadn't*. Yet, in so many ways he had. Because he was standing in front of her, with the tiniest amount of recognition in his gaze. And he'd called her Sunshine. As though he remembered her. As though he thought her worth remembering.

"I-I thought you... Well, that you..."

"Were dead?" he offered, his voice dull and monotonous. Nothing like it used to be.

"Well." She paused, knowing that Elodie would have said something kind and polite, and Hope would have just batted her lashes at him. But that had never been her style, and she saw no reason to change that now. "Yes, as it happens."

His deadened eyes flickered with surprise, and a minuscule smile even pulled at his lips. "Honesty, at least," he answered before scrutinizing her intensely. "I must admit my memory isn't what it used to be. But I think I remember that blunt honesty was a particular forte of yours."

Francesca swallowed an odd lump in her throat. Her emotions were riotous, her heart thumping painfully in her chest. She couldn't even begin to think of what to say. She had so many questions, so many confusing thoughts. Yet, right then, all she could think of was that he remembered her. On some level.

"Glad you remember," she said tartly, though her voice was gravelly to her own ears. "It will save us so much nonsensical chitchat, don't you think?"

His answering smile flickered away as quickly as it had appeared, and the silence between them grew awkward once more.

Finally, when it became unbearable, Cheska spoke again. "What happened to you, Adam? Where have you been?"

His face grew bleaker at her questions, and she knew she shouldn't be asking them, but then in her experience, she shouldn't say half of what she said.

"Why I've been to war, of course. The conquering hero." His tone was harsh enough that she flinched slightly. "And then there was the small matter of me losing my mind and most of my memories."

She didn't know what to say in the face of his bitterness, the rage that at least lit up the deadened depths of his eyes.

"But then, we shouldn't speak of such things, should we?" he asked, though she had the distinct impression the question was rhetorical. "So, the short answer is that I've been recuperating. First in Spain, then in London. And now here."

The silence in the wake of his words was fraught enough that Cheska found herself quite speechless for one of the few times in her life.

"Would you like me to leave?"

"There's that bluntness again," he said, which wasn't really an answer, so she waited it out, letting him scrutinize her. Eventually he sighed. "I'm not really looking for company," he said, matching her bluntness with his own.

She tried not to let the words sting as she raised a brow.

"Well, in that case, you've come to the wrong place," she answered. "This is Halton. Hazy memory or not, you must know that you can't come to a town like this one and *not* expect the hoards to descend. In fact, I'm surprised the gossips aren't camped outside the gates."

His lips quirked again at her comment. "I did spy someone lurking in the bushes this morning," he quipped, and his tone was so dry that it took Cheska a moment to realize he was joking.

"Ah. That will be Mrs. Carstairs. She was practically salivating with the news when she called on my mother this morning."

"Perhaps I need to increase security around here," he answered, his tone musing. "To save me from lurking busybodies and brash blondes."

Francesca gasped with faux outrage at his statement. "Did you just compare me to the old town gossip?" she demanded and was rewarded with yet another tiny smile.

"Well, at least she had the decency to talk about it behind my back," he answered, drawing close enough for her to see the heart-wrenching desolation in his green eyes. To inhale the spicy, bergamot scent that she'd never forgotten. "Whereas you just arrived unannounced to accuse me of being dead."

Though his words weren't exactly friendly, he didn't look put out by her unannounced arrival. And in fact, he was losing a tiny bit of that air of unbearable sadness.

"A thousand apologies, my lord." She tilted her chin in a manner that she hoped conveyed she wasn't sorry at all. "Next time I come to accuse you of something, I'll be sure to have your butler announce it."

At that, he barked a laugh that sounded so rusty and disused that she wondered when the last time he'd used it was. If the look of surprise in his eyes was anything to go by, it was a shock to him, too.

"So, do I invite you in for tea?" he asked. "I'm afraid I'm a little rusty around the rules of polite Society."

Francesca tipped her head to the side, studying this man that was at once familiar and a complete stranger. He looked as though he'd rather walk barefoot on hot coals than sit and have tea with her. But she wouldn't take that personally, considering she'd rather do *anything* than sit and have tea with someone.

"So am I, as it happens. And I don't have the excuse of a war for my failings."

The moment the words left her lips, she regretted them. And even more so when she saw a mask of hollow *nothingness* fall over his handsome face.

"I didn't…" she began but got no further before he interrupted her, taking a deliberate step back from her.

"Come to think of it, I'm afraid the house isn't fit for guests, Miss…"

"Templeworth," she added dully, her heart twisting at the dismissal. How could he remember that silly nickname but not her real name?

"Templeworth, yes," he spoke softly almost to himself. "Hope, was it?"

Francesca felt the very air around them still. Hope? *Hope?* Of course. Of course, he'd remember her beautiful, vivacious sister. A humiliating sort of sadness built up in her stomach, but she pushed it ruthlessly away in favor of outrage.

"No, not bloody Hope," she snapped, not caring a whit about the surprise in his eyes or the fact that she was swearing like a sailor in front of the marquess and his staff. The servants would be well used to it now in any case since they lived near her. "I'm Francesca," she continued, forcing ice into her veins and her voice. "Welcome back to Halton, my lord."

She hoped that the sarcasm in the statement was obvious as she spun on her heel and marched away from him, the sting of humiliation burning her cheeks. She had no idea why she should care so much that a man with whom she had no relationship, a man that she'd thought was dead mere hours ago, had mistaken her for her sister. But she did care.

Her head was spinning, her heart hammering with thoughts and emotions she couldn't even begin to process. Confusing thoughts. Embarrassment, yes, but also a bizarre sense of concern for him. As though she had any right to be concerned for him in the first place.

But as she stomped away, she couldn't help the worry nagging at her, and the desperate sadness that swept through her as she thought about his eyes. Once brimming with life and mischief. Now hollow and haunted and completely foreign to her.

"Well, that didn't take long. Am I to assume it didn't go well?"

Francesca wheeled around to see Sophia leaning casually against a towering oak already turning red and gold in the autumn sun.

"What are you doing here?" she groused at her sister, who skipped over to walk alongside her.

"What do you think I'm doing?" Sophia snorted, flipping her braided hair over her shoulder as they walked. "You took off from the garden as though the hounds of hell were after you. So naturally, I followed in case I missed anything exciting."

"Well, you didn't," Cheska sniffed.

"Hmm. I beg to differ. I distinctly heard you swearing at someone or something. Have I to assume that was the marquess lately returned from the grave?"

Cheska rolled her eyes at her sister but answered, nonetheless, because she knew Sophia's stubbornness was legendary, and she absolutely would not give up unless she got an answer.

"Yes, it was the marquess. No, he doesn't remember me. He did, however, remember Hope." She worked hard to keep her tone indifferent, sure that she wasn't fooling her sister. But mercifully, Sophia stayed quiet. "And he's–he's different. Not the Adam I knew. And apparently, I'm not someone he knows either."

Chapter Four

"MY LORD, SOME more invitations have arrived for you. And you have a caller."

For one mad moment, Adam thought that perhaps the forthright blonde was back. And for a moment, he felt a flickering of happiness at that. But that was foolish for a whole host of reasons. Namely, that he'd somehow managed to insult the chit.

"I'm not accepting callers," he said gruffly for what felt like the hundredth time that week, waving away the butler and his silver tray filled with yet more invitations to dinners and dances and whatever else went on in a place like Halton.

He'd assumed that Halton would be quiet and isolated after the bustle of Town. He'd thought that he could rusticate in solitude here, but Francesca Templeworth's words had proven true; there was no peace to be had for the new lord in town.

It was strange when he allowed himself to sober up long enough to think at all, that he kept circling back to *her*. Miss Templeworth. Francesca. Cheska, he'd remembered last night when he'd been ruminating over her visit yet again. The bold, headstrong girl who had been a force to be reckoned with even back then. And their brief encounter led Adam to believe that not much had changed. She was still bold and headstrong. Only now, instead of being a pretty girl, she was a devastatingly beautiful woman.

Even noticing that fact had taken Adam somewhat by surprise. How long had it been since he'd noticed anything like a woman's beauty? How long since he'd had such flowery thoughts about how her hair shone like the brightest rays of sunlight? Or how her eyes looked like pools of the clearest water? He scoffed at himself as he downed another measure of brandy, the amber liquid doing its job of numbing his bleak emotions.

"One of your callers is the local vicar, my lord. A Mr. Bell."

Adam looked back up at the butler, raising an eyebrow at the man's refusal to follow his instructions.

"So?" he asked quietly.

"I just thought perhaps…"

"Is it your job to think?" he growled.

The butler, Hodges, Adam remembered, paled and began to stammer apologies, but before he'd even gotten a coherent word out, a cacophony of other voices sounded behind the man, growing ever closer. Female, loud, and apparently completely uncaring about propriety since it seemed they'd let themselves in regardless of whether they were wanted or not.

"That seems rather rude."

"Gracious Cheska, with all your blabbering about how handsome the marquess is, you never mentioned his being a tyrant."

"Didn't you say he was nice?"

"I said nothing of the sort. He was partially polite, is what I said. And only when he thought I was you, Hope."

"Lady Claremont, Miss Templeworth, please. I do not think…"

"Mr. Bell, do be quiet."

"Sophia! Don't be so rude to the vicar."

"Why not? He's family, isn't he? Gideon is always insulting him."

Adam rose to his feet, shock rendering him unable to do anything but stare as four ladies and a red-faced young man barreled through the door. His eyes felt as though they were on stalks as he took in the unwanted company. The two brunettes and the other blonde. And of course, the firecracker from the other day. He felt a jolt of something like pleasure at seeing her, but from the way her chin was tilted mutinously upward, and those deep, blue eyes were flashing, he could guess that the feeling wasn't mutual.

And come to think of it, he shouldn't be in any way pleased to see her since she'd essentially broken into his house with this rabid mob. Hodges staggered in after them, sweat breaking out beneath his shock of white hair, which he flattened against his head with a trembling hand.

"M-my lord, I…"

"Don't blame the butler for our unwelcome presence," Francesca piped up without even a hint of demureness in her tone or expression. "He's not the first we've managed to outrun, and I doubt he'll be the last."

Adam didn't quite know what to say in response. What to make of this insane beauty before him surrounded by her equally mad cohorts. He took his time taking them all in, scowling in the hopes that they'd be deterred. But by the looks of it, Francesca Templeworth's fire was a family trait, for not one of the ladies cowered or even blinked. The only person in the room visibly flushed and shaking was the vicar. And Hodges.

Adam ran his gaze over the ladies before him, all of them uncommonly pretty, and memories flickered in his mind. Memories of dancing and laughing and being young and carefree. All things that were as alien to him now as being the Marquess of Heywood. The two brunettes were a study in opposites, the older dark-eyed and perfectly put together. The younger's eyes were similar to Francesca's, and her loose hair and breeches were decidedly *not* perfectly put together.

The blonde, the one called Hope, he now realized, was as lovely as he remembered with her golden curls, darker than Francesca's bright blonde, and her deep brown eyes sparkling with a mischief that he remembered well. He also remembered having something of a boyhood infatuation with her, thinking she was the most beautiful girl he'd ever seen. Yet now, while there was no denying she was beautiful, as they all were, she didn't hold the appeal of her sister. The sister who was already drawing his gaze again.

The silence was excruciating, and Adam realized that they were all expecting him to break it. His heart ratcheted up, and his palms grew clammy as they all stared at him. This was why he didn't want callers. This was why he never should have been the damned marquess. He wasn't cut out for this. He didn't *want* this.

Panic and that anger that always lurked within him nowadays, and the brandy he'd been consuming, swirled into a maelstrom inside him.

"What do you want?" he barked, unwilling and unable to temper his tone. Why should he care about manners in any case since his companions clearly cared not a whit about them?

"Charming."

"Hush, Sophia."

"Why? He's not exactly pleasant, is he?"

"Yes well, we're not exactly welcome either, so it's not unreasonable to be…"

"We don't want anything from you."

Francesca Templeworth's blunt statement rang out clear as a bell amongst her sisters' less-than-subtle whisperings, and Adam felt his ire rise. They'd barreled in here unannounced and uninvited, almost killed his poor butler by the sounds of the man's wheezing, and now she was snapping at him as though displeased with *his* behavior. The chit was mad. They all were.

"But Mr. Bell is insisting on meeting you, why, I have no idea since I already told him of your abrasiveness, but there we have it. A man of the cloth and all that. And since he was too scared to face you alone, we decided to help. Well, *I* decided to help. My sisters are just being nosy."

"Actually, I'm being a dutiful sister-in-law and offering my help to Kit," the other blonde announced.

"And I'm here to make sure you all behave. Though frankly, I've already given that up as a lost cause," the older brunette said wryly.

He didn't know why, but Adam turned then to the last of them, thinking she was bound to have something to add. And sure enough, she shrugged and spoke up. "I am actually just being nosy," she said frankly.

"L-lord Heywood, I didn't mean, that is to say, I wouldn't have... We shouldn't..."

"Oh, for heaven's sake Kit, sit down before you faint. He's trying to say that he never would have dared to face your wrath if we hadn't forced him to."

"And why did you feel the need to force him to? I thought I made my disinterest in visitors clear." He quite forgot they had a room full of spectators as he stared down the tiny ball of ire going toe to toe with him.

"Oh, you did, believe me," she bit back. "But call me sentimental, I actually wanted to help you."

"And this helps me how, exactly?"

She rolled her eyes and sighed, squeezing the bridge of her nose and mumbling something about obstinate males, which though he couldn't hear it clearly was certain to be an insult.

"Because Mr. Bell here is one of the few people in this village who is calling on you with good intentions and not because he's simply *dying* to run to the rest of the vultures to gossip about you. He is sincere in his offer of friendship."

He opened his mouth to respond, but she didn't give him the opportunity. "And in all honesty, the chances are that we will be in each other's social circles should you ever decide to leave your cave here. The Earl of Claremont is Mr. Bell's brother and Hope's husband. And Elle is the Viscountess of Brentford. That means that whether you want to be around us or not, at some stage, you'll probably have to be."

"I won't have to be around anyone if I choose to stay in my home," he countered through gritted teeth. "Undisturbed," he added with a scowl at the still-wheezing servant by the door.

The derisive snort from one of the siblings interrupted him, and he glared at the assembled Templeworths and their unwilling co-conspirator. But they all remained impressively if not annoyingly unperturbed by his anger.

"Good luck with the undisturbed part, Lord Heywood." Adam tried not to wince at the title that he still wasn't used to. But if Lady Claremont noticed, she didn't give any indication of doing so. "Trust me when I tell you that the residents of Halton will get to you one way or another. I should know," she added wryly.

"Your sister said as much," he answered grudgingly.

"Yes, but she probably wasn't as polite about it as I'm being," she answered with a dimpled smile.

"I…" Adam began but drew to an immediate halt because truth be told, he had absolutely no idea what to say to these madwomen. He should ask them to sit and offer refreshments. But he wouldn't because he didn't *want* them to sit and have refreshments, and so when the awkward silence grew again, he did nothing to break it.

After an age, Lady Brentford, who definitely seemed to be the peacemaker of the ladies, spoke up. "Perhaps we should leave the marquess to his…"

"Grumpiness?"

"Drinking?"

"Wallowing?"

Adam felt his jaw drop at the three termagants as they reeled off insults toward him.

"To his affairs," Lady Brentford said firmly and with such practiced patience that he just knew this wasn't the first time she'd had to corral the little tearaways. Surely as a married woman, the countess should be conducting herself in a far less scandalous fashion?

The poor vicar looked as though his legs would give out as he stepped forward to offer a wobbly bow. "We do apologize, my lord, for imposing upon you so. I wished to invite you to dine with me. Or us, rather. A-at the vicarage this evening or when it is convenient," he stammered nervously.

Adam was about to turn him down, naturally, when the bold Miss Francesca piped up.

"You are quite wasting your time, Kit. Can't you see he'd rather stick pins in his eyes than deign to socialize with any of us? Come along, we'll dine with you instead."

They all turned to go, offering stilted bows and curtsies, except for Francesca, who stuck her nose up at him and spun around in a flurry of sky-blue skirts toward the door.

And he had no idea what possessed him to do it. He was free and clear, no obligations, no threat of unwanted company foisted upon him. But something about that chit and her impertinence riled him enough to call out before she dragged the reverend out of earshot.

"Mr. Bell."

As one, the group of unexpected visitors turned to face him.

"Thank you for the invitation," he said. "I should be happy to accept. I'll see you all this evening."

Though he spoke to the lot of them, he trained his eyes on Francesca, noting the glint of fire in her gaze with a perverse sort of satisfaction. She ignored him, however, as she turned and continued to stomp out of his house.

Just as he ignored his butler's shocked expression as Adam swept by him and went to ready himself for a dinner he wasn't sure he wanted to attend.

Chapter Five

"WHAT WILL YOU wear tonight to dazzle the maudlin marquess?"

Cheska rolled her eyes at Hope, who swept into her bedchamber looking as beautiful as ever in gold damask. Usually, Francesca didn't mind that Hope looked like a china doll come to life. But since Adam had called *her* Hope, she had to admit that it grated just a little. Which was foolish in the extreme because for one thing, Cheska had never cared about such things, and for another, it wasn't as though Hope was that beautiful to spite the rest of them.

And besides, she was completely and utterly besotted with her extremely possessive husband. Gideon still gritted his teeth at the fawning Hope received, even after all this time. Christian wasn't much better with Elodie, truth be told. Elodie who now arrived in a confection of dusky silk.

"I do hope you're going to wear your blue silk, Cheska. The color is so becoming on you," Elodie said as she rummaged through the wardrobe and pulled the dress loose.

"Indeed, and it makes your figure positively eye-popping," Hope snickered, ignoring Elodie's half-hearted protestations.

"And whose eyes do you suppose I should be trying to pop?" Cheska asked. "It's only going to be us and the marquess. Hardly a Society ball."

"My dear, one must always try one's best to pop eyes should

the situation arise. If only for entertainment," Hope answered with a grin. "Besides, if this afternoon's visit was anything to go by, Adam Fairchild's eyes are very much in danger of popping."

"Yes, I'd imagine they are," Cheska agreed. "But only because his head is likely to explode with temper. Couldn't you see how much he hated us all being there?"

"There is a thin line between hate and love, Cheska. A *very* thin line. Trust me."

"Elle, talk some sense into her, will you?" she appealed to her sister who was instructing the abigail to take the gown down to be pressed.

"Usually I would, but in this instance, she's right, Cheska. Passion is passion, after all, and sometimes anger and hate can slip toward something more—"

"Scandalous. Wicked. Positively delicious," Hope supplied unhelpfully.

When they were younger, Francesca used to dread marriage, thinking it would turn her into a meek, biddable, boring nitwit. Someone who tolerated her husband's presence in her life when he decided to snap his fingers for her to come running.

But her sisters' marriages were nothing like that. Nothing at all. They were worshipped like goddesses by their respective husbands. Shamelessly and absolutely. So much so that Elodie had come out of her shell and even developed a personality. And Hope, rather than become stiff and missish, had grown infinitely more outlandish and shameless. It didn't help that Gideon not only loved that about his wife but even encouraged it.

And Christian was no better with Elodie. He'd made her a veritable wanton and was thoroughly delighted by that if his constant expression of male smugness was anything to go by.

And ordinarily, Francesca loved that for her sisters and admired her brothers-in-law for eschewing the normal way of things in the *beau monde* and actually showing affection for their wives.

But not when it led those wives to stand in her bedchamber and talk about Adam Fairchild and her in such terms.

"Need I remind you that the man thought I was you, Hope?" Francesca asked, a little snippily. "Or that he was unpardonably rude to all of us and most vociferously against spending any time with us?"

"Oh, stuff and nonsense. The man's been away for years, Cheska. Not to mention to *war* and back."

"A war that took the life of his brother," Elle interjected gently.

"Quite," Hope said with a nod. "You can hardly blame him for a hazy memory after all that. And honestly, it's a slow day when someone *isn't* unpardonably rude to us, as you well know."

"But…"

"And," Elle joined in. "He might have been against dining with Kit, but he did agree to it. Because of you."

Francesca felt her cheeks heat, and she grew slightly flustered. Something that was alien to her. "It absolutely was not because of me," she insisted. "If anything, it was in spite of me."

She looked up from the gloves she'd been fiddling with to see both her sisters smiling at her in an annoyingly knowing way.

"What?" she demanded.

"Oh, nothing," Elodie said as she glided toward the door, graceful as a swan. "It's just that line we spoke of? Between love and hate?"

"What about it?"

"It just seems as though you and the marquess are set to walk it," Hope said before darting out of the room after Elodie, not giving Cheska a chance to answer. Which was just as well, she thought, fidgeting with the gloves again, since she had no idea what to say.

SHE WAS NOT watching the door. She was absolutely, categorically *not* watching for Adam Fairchild's arrival, Francesca told herself as she once again looked at the longcase clock in the corner of Kit's drawing room.

He likely wouldn't come in any case. He certainly didn't *want* to. He'd agreed as some sort of one-up on her, though she couldn't care less if he attended or not. Truth be told, she'd much rather prefer a quiet, family dinner. Papa was still bedbound from his illness, but they wouldn't exactly feel his absence since he rarely attended social events with them. In fact, he rarely ate with them at home if he could help it, choosing instead to take trays in his study or library.

So, it made absolutely no difference to Francesca if the sullen Adam Fairchild didn't turn up.

Her thoughts were interrupted by the arrival of the marquess, and her heart stumbled as her eyes were drawn to him. He looked outrageously handsome, she decided, as she raked her gaze over him.

It was so often the case that her brothers-in-law towered over every gentleman in the room that she was surprised to see Adam stood as tall as Gideon and only slightly shorter than Christian. His deep, green jacket was only a shade or two darker than his startling eyes and was the perfect foil to his sandy hair. And lord, but the man could fill out a jacket! She could barely take her eyes off the breadth of his shoulders, and when she did, it was only to admire the obvious strength in his thighs, evidenced by the skintight breeches he wore.

"Who are you ogling?"

Francesca jumped at the sound of Sophia's voice in her ear, and she turned to glower at her sister looking uncomfortable in a pale lemon gown.

"I'm not ogling anybody, thank you very much." She sniffed, though she couldn't help but glance his way again. Kit had been joined in his efforts by Gideon and Christian, and Francesca felt a sudden and unexpected pang of sympathy for Adam, who looked painfully uncomfortable, though he did at least seem to be answering their questions.

"No, that's definitely an ogle," Sophia said matter-of-factly.

"Who's ogling?"

"Bloody hell," Cheska swore as she glared at Hope, who'd arrived at her other shoulder. "Be quiet. They'll hear you."

"Who will?"

"Adam. Kit. Everyone."

"So?"

"So perhaps it's not the most proper topic of conversation at a dinner party?" This from Elle, who popped up behind her. Honestly, were they all just waiting in corners to pounce on her? It certainly felt so.

"Oh, who cares?" said Hope, the image of nonchalance. "Never let a silly thing like propriety get in the way of a good ogling. That's what I always say."

Francesca snorted while Elodie sighed behind them. Ordinarily, she would be in full support of a good ogling. But for some reason, she would rather stick pins in her eyes than be caught staring at Adam Fairchild. The man who hadn't remembered her and then had thought she was her sister.

She was just considering giving up entirely and sneaking out the back when suddenly, Adam looked straight at her, and her gaze was caught in the striking green of his own. Francesca felt as though the world around her fell away. Or at least she did until Sophia's voice sounded in her ear. In the loudest whisper possible.

"I think you have some competition in the ogling stakes, Cheska. And by the looks of things, the marquess doesn't have the same problem with it as you do."

Chapter Six

"WE WERE SO sorry to hear of the dear Lord Heywood's passing, my lord. And of course, your brother. How tragic."

Adam winced at the faux concern in Mrs. Templeworth's nasally voice. He'd gotten well used to people who pretended to be offering condolences whilst sniffing out tidbits of gossip like bloodhounds. And she was up there with the worst of them. And that wasn't even starting in on the fact that his father could have been described as many things, but dear wasn't one of them. Besides, the old marquess had been an insufferable snob and never would have given his time or attention to an untitled, country family. But Mrs. Templeworth was obviously the type that wouldn't let a silly thing like truth get in the way of hunting out a morsel of information to share with the other rabid vultures in this town.

The only consolation, if it could even be considered so, was that he'd been so damned distracted by the woman's daughter all evening that he barely registered most of her vulgarity. And as he looked again—inevitably—at Francesca Templeworth and saw her shoot daggers at her mother down the dinner table. He couldn't help but feel a tiny burst of warmth in his long-dead heart.

She was shrewd beyond anyone he'd ever met, so he had no doubt that she knew exactly what her odious mother was about, and by the looks of things, she was almost as disgusted by it as he was.

"The venison is lovely, Kit," Francesca said, turning her gaze to the vicar. "Your cook is improving."

That burst of warmth grew hotter at her obvious attempt to change the subject, and she threw a fleeting look of apology his way. Adam could only wonder at such a woman as Mrs. Templeworth raising a girl like Francesca. Then, he looked around the table at the other three Templeworth girls, who launched into a conversation about the food and laughingly shared anecdotes of the cook's apparent mishaps over the years. Kit, they said, had been too kind-hearted to get rid of the woman, even when she'd almost poisoned him for a month straight.

They discussed it in loud and long detail. So much so that their mother, despite her clear efforts to interrupt, was drowned out at every turn. And another glance toward Francesca proved that they were doing it on purpose. Even the earl and the viscount seemed to be in on it since he'd spoken to both gentlemen earlier, and neither seemed particularly interested in the vicar's cuisine.

Adam let the chatter wash over him, surprising himself by even laughing quietly once or twice at some of the more imaginative descriptions of past meals. The Templeworth ladies were certainly elaborate in their descriptions, and he found, shockingly, that he might even be enjoying himself. Just a little.

But it wasn't long before the audacious matriarch of the Templeworths reared her head again, and no sooner was there a lull in the conversation than she pounced.

"We had heard, Lord Heywood, that you yourself might have died at war. Imagine our surprise when the news broke that not only was the new marquess arriving in Halton but that it was *you* and not some distant cousin or nephew. Why, I said to my dear friend Mrs. Carstairs—"

"I remember when Hope tried to bake those pies and I cast up my accounts all over the dining table."

Francesca's blurted statement brought an immediate cessation to the talk. Even Mrs. Templeworth's. Adam gazed at her in amazement, then snorted a laugh at her quick wink in his direction.

"How dare you? I slaved over those pies, you ungrateful little shrew," Lady Claremont laughingly objected. "And if I remember correctly, *your* apple tarts almost killed us all."

"You were not ill because of those apple tarts, Hope Templeworth-Bell. You were ill because you were pregnant," Francesca declared, and Adam could only gape at such open talk in front of gentlemen. Most especially him. Indeed, Mrs. Templeworth let out a ghastly cry and looked as though she would faint clean away. Lady Brentford dropped her head into her hands as she muttered to herself.

"Francesca." Mrs. Templeworth sounded as though she were being strangled as she cast her eyes down the table, the expression in them a mix of horror, reproach, and desperate pleading. "You must not speak of such things in company. You *know* this. I've *told* you this."

Adam flicked his eyes between the two ladies in fascination. But as he suspected would be the case, Francesca Templeworth seemed completely unconcerned about her mother's admonishments.

"Oh please, I'm sure everyone here knows how babes are made, Mama. Even the bachelors." She looked down the table to the vicar, who was an alarming shade of puce and then to Adam, her blue eyes wide and deceptively innocent. "Lord Heywood, are you familiar with the workings of human procreation?"

Adam could only stare at the little hoyden across the table and because he was staring, he saw the flicker of challenge in her eyes. The glint of mischief. No doubt, she took great enjoyment in being scandalous. To the detriment of her mother's health, it seemed, as the older lady paled significantly, even as the poor vicar's cheeks grew impossibly redder.

"Cheska, you're going to kill Kit if you don't behave yourself," Lady Brentford scolded, though Adam couldn't help but notice that she was gazing at him expectantly, too. As if to see how he'd react.

It had been years since Adam had been the focus of anyone's attention. Let alone a tableful of mad people. But he found himself loathe to back away from the light of challenge in Miss Francesca Templeworth's eyes. And so, when she raised a brow at him, he raised one right back.

"I am extremely familiar with how procreation works, Sunshine," he said with a rarely used smirk. "And quite fond of it, too. Or at least the practice of it."

Another wail sounded from the direction of Mrs. Templeworth, but Adam kept his eyes fixed on Francesca. Somehow, it seemed as though they'd gotten themselves into some sort of battle of wills, and he'd be damned if he'd be the first to look away. He'd been hoping that she'd blush and stammer and shy away from his scandalous words. But he should have known better given who he was dealing with. And she didn't take long in disabusing him of that foolish notion, for her mouth widened in a grin of pure devilment. "Men usually are. Or so I'm told."

The lust that slammed into him as he took in the expression on her face took Adam by surprise, and he felt his shoulders stiffen at the unfamiliar sensation. It wasn't as though he were some green lad who fell apart at the sight of a pretty smile. But it had been so long since he'd felt anything other than despair, anger, guilt, he wasn't quite sure what to do with the emotion. He barely registered the ribald talk of the two other lords at the table. The cackling of one of their wives and the blushing admonishments of the other. The older woman's laments and the vicar's valiant yet useless attempts to steer the conversation back to some modicum of decency. All he could think of, all he could feel really, was that unwelcome desire for the woman across the table and the panic that came with it.

But before he could act on the foolish temptation to run, Sophia Templeworth, who'd been largely quiet, spoke up.

"Much as I'm sure your fondness for the act of procreation is absolutely riveting, Lord Heywood, I couldn't help but notice that marvelous stallion of yours in your stables. And I am simply dying to know more about him."

The chit's words succeeded in distracting him from his anxiety. Not least because the only way she'd notice Ares would be if she'd gone snooping around his stables. Something that he absolutely wouldn't put past her now that he'd gotten to know her a little.

"I should very much like to ride him. He looks at least sixteen hands!"

"Sophia, you cannot invite yourself onto someone else's horse," Lady Brentford said in the tone of someone well used to trying to control the incorrigible girl.

"Of course, I can't, Elle, I'm not a savage," the brunette retorted with a roll of her eyes. "I'm going to wait for *him* to invite me."

And once again, Adam found them all looking expectantly at him. Oh, they were good. Manipulative but good. They had to know, given how rude he'd been when they broke into his house, that he absolutely did not want visitors. Especially on his horses. Perhaps she was relying on good manners to get her access to Ares. Well, she was out of luck because manners were something Adam had never paid attention to. Especially since the war.

But somehow, after this evening in their company, after watching Francesca jump to his rescue again and again, even while she challenged him and dared him to engage in whatever game she was playing, he found himself not wanting to say no.

"Of course, you couldn't possibly go alone. When he invites you, I mean. You can't go visiting single gentlemen all by yourself. Even if everyone else is too scared to go near him to see you there." This from Lady Claremont who blinked innocently when he locked eyes on her.

"No, she certainly cannot," Lord Brentford said. Growled, really. It seemed that with Mr. Templeworth out of action, the viscount had put himself into the position of protector for the girls. And Adam found that he was rather pleased to hear that since they damn well needed watching. Closely.

"Well then, Cheska can go with her," Lady Claremont announced, beaming at them all.

Adam felt a jolt of pleasure at the countess's words, though he kept his face neutral.

"That's hardly better, love," Lord Claremont said, his dark eyes boring into Adam, who resisted the urge to pull at his cravat.

"And why is that?" Francesca asked in a haughty tone that screamed danger. But the earl merely grinned at her.

"Because, sister dear, you are quite possibly the worst behaved of all of you, which is terrifying but also true," the earl drawled, wrapping an arm around the countess, who sank back against him, uncaring that they were at dinner. Uncaring that it was the exact opposite of how ton spouses were supposed to behave. But then he glanced at the viscount, who had just seconds ago been playing the overprotective man but was now nuzzling his wife's neck as though she were the next course.

"Be that as it may, I'm perfectly capable of making sure the marquess doesn't try to have his way with my sister."

Adam, who'd just taken a sip of his claret, almost choked to death at her words. She was a bloody nuisance! She should be gagged and locked away somewhere.

"I can assure you, madam, I have no nefarious intentions toward your sister," he spat through gritted teeth, aware that everyone was once again staring at him. But he only had eyes for the pest across the table.

"Why?" she asked, her voice dripping with faux sweetness. "Because she's not Hope?"

The silence after her question was deafening, and Adam sensed more than saw the earl stiffen in his seat.

Was the chit trying to get him killed? Had he really insulted her so by using the wrong damned name *once* after so many years of being away? And on the heel of his anger at her outrageous question came the thought; if she *was* that angry about it, then why? After all, she'd spent the dinner risking her mother's ire time and again to save him from awkward conversations about his past, about the war, and the decimation of his family. So why act like this now when her sister practically blackmailed him into letting her at his prized stallion?

Might she be jealous? The idea clanged through his head before he could stop it. As did a shocking sort of pleasure at the idea of her being jealous. He'd felt more emotions in the last two days than he had in years. And all because of the lady with the serpent's tongue sitting across from him.

Why the notion should please him, Adam couldn't begin to understand. But he couldn't deny being intrigued by the idea. He shouldn't engage in any sort of back and forth with her. Not with her entire family watching them. Not when he had little to no interest in conversing with *anyone,* let alone a woman who was already driving him mad. Not with her two guard dogs practically snarling at them. Especially Claremont thanks to Francesca's little trick.

But instead of taking his leave, he found himself grinning across at her.

"Perhaps it's because she's not you," he said softly and earned himself a gasp of stunned outrage from Mrs. Templeworth to match the ones she leveled at her daughters.

Chapter Seven

"I THOUGHT YOU were going to wait to be invited?" Francesca watched from the stable doors as Sophia finished mucking out her mare's stable, then stomped toward her, brushing excess hay from her palms.

"No, Elodie said I *couldn't* invite myself, and then I said I'd wait. But frankly, two days is long enough, and if you'll remember, he's not exactly the most welcoming of town inhabitants, so if we wait any longer, the horse will be dead and buried before I even get to pat it."

Francesca laughed at Sophia's dramatics, but her stomach was still doing that odd flip it did any time she thought of Adam Fairchild.

It was just, ordinarily, she'd be leading the charge on one of their schemes or adventures. And she'd never usually let a thing like not being invited get in her way. But after that dinner... After that final comment, in that low growl of his, well, she felt on edge around him.

Not quite herself. Of course, she hadn't let him see that. She'd merely snorted whilst Mama rounded them all up and dragged them home, bemoaning her lot in life to be cursed with such horrible daughters. Or something to that effect. In truth, Cheska had barely been listening. She rarely listened to her mother anyway if she could help it.

But it had been so difficult to school her features into a look of derision. So difficult to keep a cool countenance, while inside her heart was thundering at an alarming speed. She'd been acting like a complete ninny, and it had annoyed her. Why, only days ago, she'd thought him dead. Then he'd been really quite rude to her.

"Cheska, are you even listening?"

Sophia's impatient tone interrupted what was turning into quite the wanton wool-gathering, and Cheska dragged her mind back to the matter at hand. It was one bloody comment! She'd had far more flirtatious comments from men before, far more scandalous, and lecherous propositions than an invitation to a stable. He'd been trying to rattle her, that was all.

She'd seen the irritation in Adam's eyes when she'd implied that he was interested in Hope. For some reason, she kept falling into odd battles of wills with him. And Hope's husband wasn't pleased about it either.

"Cheska was just trying to rile him up, my love," Hope had assured him with a pat on the hand as they'd rumbled home from the vicarage. "She was hurt that he'd *once* misremembered her name after years of being away and going through the many horrors of war."

Francesca had felt about an inch tall at the obvious condemnation in Hope's tone. But hell would freeze over before she would admit it, so she'd merely tilted her chin and stared Hope down until the carriage had stopped and Gideon dragged his wife inside to make good on her promises.

"I can smack you if you think it will help you focus. It would be my pleasure."

Once again, Sophia's voice interrupted Cheska's wandering thoughts, and she managed to duck just in time to avoid being smacked by a leather riding glove.

"I can't believe you were truly going to strike me," she snapped at her sister, who shrugged nonchalantly.

"Are you coming or not?" Sophia demanded.

"Not," Cheska bit, still slightly sulking from the near smack.

Still slightly nervous from her last encounter with the marquess.

"Very well, I'll see you when I get back," Sophia said as she took a few steps toward the gate that led to a shortcut across the meadows. "Funny," she called over her shoulder. "I never thought you a coward."

And Francesca knew, she *knew* that Sophia was just trying to annoy her. But it worked. And before Sophia had slipped through the gate, Cheska was running to catch up to her.

"OH, ISN'T HE positively divine?"

Adam heard the unmistakably female voice coming from the stable and knew that at least one of the Templeworths had decided that waiting for an actual invitation was beyond her capabilities. And rather than be annoyed by that, he found himself amused.

Just as he had twenty minutes ago when his stablemaster had requested an urgent meeting in his study to inform him that he'd found a young lady in Ares's stable and didn't know what to do with her. The man had looked so shocked by Adam's laugh that he felt a twinge of guilt. Had he really been so monstrous that one laugh was that unusual? And the truth was that yes, he had.

Adam had made quick work of assuring the old master that he'd take care of their visitor, then quickly made his way to the stables, ignoring what felt very much like disappointment that the servant had mentioned *one* surprise visitor and not two.

He'd known that nobody in that family would patiently await a formal invitation, and he'd found himself enjoying the waiting game to see how long they'd take to break. He knew that if his horse had already been accosted, then it was the youngest Templeworth in his stables. But he couldn't stop wishing that...

"I mean, he's a horse, Sophia. But a very nice one."

Adam's heart stalled, then galloped. She had come after all.

The shrew who looked like sunshine. He paused long enough to straighten his charcoal riding jacket, then continued, making sure to keep his steps quiet and unhurried.

"You just don't appreciate good horseflesh like me," Sophia's voice carried out to him, sounding appalled by that fact.

"Sophia, nobody in Christendom appreciates horseflesh like you," came the droll reply. "But rest assured, I think he's as good a horse as any I've seen. There. Will that do?"

He heard the younger one's sigh even from out here. "Why did you even come if you don't care about the horses?" Adam paused again, holding his breath for the answer, which was unexpectedly important to him. Would she say it was because she wanted to see him? Did he even *want* that to be her answer? His mind was still so mixed up, his thoughts still so dark and painful, he knew he still wasn't ready to want someone in his life. But in all his years of misery, she had been the only bright spot in the last few days. Even though she seemed perpetually annoyed at him.

While he was trying to figure out his confusing feelings, she promptly disabused him of the notion that she was there for him.

"I came because you threatened me with bodily harm, you little brat. And since the marquess is nowhere to be seen, and the stable workers don't seem inclined to toss you out on your backside, I'm going to walk down to the river. I'll give you thirty minutes before I start walking home without you. And don't try to steal any of his horses," she tacked on in a no-nonsense tone. "Remember how annoyed Christian got when you took that pair of greys?"

Adam found himself holding in a laugh. He could just imagine the horse-mad Sophia taking off with her brother-in-law's horses. Brentford and Claremont must have the patience of saints to deal with this on a regular basis.

"Stay out of trouble," came the response, which was ironic since from the little Adam knew of the family, Miss Sophia was quite as likely to go looking for trouble as her sister.

"Stay away from criminal activities," came the response. And then after a brief pause, Francesca spoke again. "Or at least, don't get caught."

My God, they were unbelievable! He'd never met anyone like them.

Before he took another step, he spotted Francesca's bright golden curls as she swept from the stable, and he found himself not heading inside as he'd intended but, instead, watching her hurry through the gardens in the direction of the river. He watched the sway of her hips in her long-sleeved, periwinkle gown, a nod to the crispier weather they'd been having of late. And then scoffed at himself for noticing such a thing as a lady's fashion. But it wasn't the dress that held his attention, it was what was inside of it. And once again, that desire flowed through his veins. And without conscious thought, his feet carried him after Francesca.

Chapter Eight

"ARE YOU GOING to make it a habit to invite yourself to my property, Sunshine?"

Francesca whirled around at the sound of Adam's voice behind her. He was leaning against one of the trees by the riverbank. Francesca, who didn't have an artistic bone in her body, suddenly wished that she had a talent for sketching so she could capture how obscenely handsome he looked standing in the afternoon sun.

And given the fact that she'd never been prone to such nonsensical drivel before, that took her quite by surprise.

But of course, she wouldn't give any hint that he was nearly rendering her speechless, so she merely shrugged her shoulders, appearing as blasé as possible.

"Only if you make it a habit to not follow through on promised invitations, my lord," she said airily. "And you should count yourself lucky that I'm here in any case. Otherwise, my sister might have absconded with one of your animals."

"I do count myself lucky that you're here," he said softly, and Francesca's stomach flipped at the words even though she knew he probably didn't mean them.

"I thought you didn't want visitors."

"So did I," he answered in that same tone that made her unsure about what to do with herself.

"And now? You've suddenly decided to integrate yourself into lofty echelons of Halton society?" she quipped, laughing as his eyes widened in horror. His eyes which she noticed were no longer quite as bleak, quite as haunted as they had been when he'd first arrived a week ago.

"God forbid," he retorted, the hint of a smile playing around his mouth. "But considering I survived a dinner with your unorthodox family, I think perhaps dealing with just one of you won't be so bad."

"Ah, yes," she agreed sagely. "If one can survive an evening of Templeworths, one can survive anything."

To her surprise, rather than laugh, he flinched slightly, and his expression grew shuttered again. She didn't know what she could have said to cause such a reaction. But as the silence grew stilted, she thought of his life before his sensational return to the village, and she could have kicked herself. Joking about survival to a war hero was not only insensitive but utterly idiotic. Especially since he'd lost his brother in that same war. And was now the marquess when she knew, perhaps better than anyone, that he'd never wanted that for himself.

"I'm sorry," she blurted. He merely gazed at her with that same desolate, almost vacant expression. "I'm so sorry for what you must have gone through. You told me once that I shouldn't wish for war. You were right. I cannot imagine what you must have experienced. I cannot imagine how lonely it must have felt, how devastating to lose Douglas. Then your father. I just…" She shrugged helplessly, not quite finding the words but needing to say something, nonetheless. "I am well aware that I am a privileged and rather coddled person. And so, I cannot say I understand, but I can say with all sincerity that I am truly sorry for all your losses and all the pain I'm sure you've experienced since I saw you last."

He didn't speak. Didn't move. Didn't react in any way, and she felt so foolish for babbling the way she had that she could feel her cheeks heat.

When it didn't look as though he'd do anything but ignore

her, she hurried past him, intending to grab hold of Sophia and drag her home to where Cheska could feel ashamed in peace. But she'd taken no more than two steps before he was upon her, grasping hold of her arm in one hand and tilting her chin up to face him with the other.

Francesca could do nothing but search his face, looking for a hint, some clue as to what he was feeling. But she saw nothing. And just as she was about to pull herself from his grip, the hand at her chin moved to cup the back of her neck, and she was pulled against him before his lips descended to capture her own in a heart-stopping kiss.

THIS WAS A mistake. A catastrophic mistake. Adam knew this, and yet the second he felt Francesca's capitulation and felt her breathy sigh against his lips, he was lost. It had been so long since he'd felt a desire like this if he ever even had. So long since he'd felt anything other than terror, angst, and grief. Yet holding this maddening, insane, beautiful woman in his arms felt like awakening from a nightmare.

The citrus scent of her wove around him as he moved his hand from her arm to her waist and pulled her closer still. Her gasp of surprise was the opening he needed to plunge his tongue inside her mouth to tangle with her own, and he couldn't help his growl of pleasure as she mirrored his movements and pushed her hips into the hardness of his aching cock. The moan that fell from her mouth into his own almost undid him there and then. Adam knew he was in very real danger of losing his tenuous grip on control.

His hands plunged into her hair, knocking pins free, and sending the golden strands of silk falling over his hand. He was going up in flames, and from the sounds she was making, he was pulling her straight into the inferno with him.

Her smart mouth had been haunting his already broken dreams all week, and now that he'd tasted her, he knew the affliction, the desire, the *need* would only grow in strength. He turned them so that her back was to the tree on which he'd been leaning, pushing forward so that she was flush against him, relishing how it pushed her even closer until nothing but their clothing separated them.

Adam wrenched his lips from her own only to move them to her jaw, her neck, nipping and licking the skin that tasted as good as it smelled. He'd take her right here against his tree. He didn't give a damn about consequences or decency. Didn't give a damn that they might be caught. He didn't give a damn about anything but being inside her.

Her fingers gripped his hair, her breathing sounded as labored as his own, and he knew she wanted him as much as he wanted her. It would be so easy to take what she was offering, he told himself fiercely. And if they were seen, well, she could do worse than a marquess for a husband if that was the outcome.

The thought was like being doused in a bucket of iced water and gave Adam the strength to pull away from her, his chest heaving as he tried to catch his breath. He clenched his hands into fists to keep from reaching for her. She was exquisite. With her golden curls and wide, blue eyes, she looked like a goddess, and he still wanted her to the point of pain.

But to shackle her to one such as he? A broken, damaged shell of the man he should have been? He would never be so unspeakably cruel to ask that of any woman. Especially not this one.

"Francesca," he whispered at the same time as she spoke.

"Adam, I…"

"Cheska! There you are."

Sophia Templeworth's voice rang out over the meadow, and Adam stumbled back from where he still stood tantalizingly close to Cheska. He couldn't tear his eyes from her, his mind a maelstrom of emotions, even when she turned her head toward her sister.

"Lord Heywood, that beast of yours is a work of art. But I must tell you, your stablehands are a little overzealous in their duties. I wasn't going to *steal* him. Just borrow him for a while."

It took a moment for Adam's head to clear enough to register what Miss Templeworth was saying, and he finally turned to see her standing before them, arms crossed, glaring at him.

"You were trying to *borrow* my stallion?" he asked, not quite distracted enough to move away from her sister.

"For a while. Honestly, you men and your possessiveness."

Adam couldn't even appreciate the oddness of the younger Templeworth since he couldn't concentrate on anything right then except Francesca.

"We should go," she mumbled, refusing to meet his eyes, and he wanted to reach out and make her look at him but of course, he wouldn't. Not least because he had no idea what to say or how to even feel right then.

But he did know that he couldn't leave things like this between them. Just as he knew that regardless of how conflicted he was feeling, and how much he'd wanted to hide away from the entire world only days ago, he didn't want Francesca Templeworth out of his life.

Damn, but he needed a drink.

He watched in tense silence as she scurried over to her sister and began dragging her away.

"Miss Sophia," he called before they could leave, before he even knew quite what he was about. "Ares is not an easy mount to handle, but if you'd like to call tomorrow, I can make him available to you."

The screech that emanated from the girl could have raised the dead, and Adam couldn't contain a surprised chuckle as she launched herself at him and threw her arms around his neck.

"Oh, *thank you*," she gasped. "Thank you, thank you, *thank you*."

Adam felt a surge of fondness toward her when he saw how thrilled something so simple made her. He was a little worried of course. Most gentlemen of his acquaintance would struggle to handle the beast. But he would be close by, and he had a feeling that a Templeworth lady could do pretty much anything she set her mind to.

He looked over at Francesca and felt his heart squeeze at the indulgent smile she was aiming at her sister. It softened her, that smile. Made her appear less hard. But when she turned her eyes back to him, a mask of cool indifference fell into place. And Adam realized that he wanted to see that smile again.

"Of course, I know it wouldn't be proper to have you arrive alone," he continued casually, keeping his eyes on Francesca. "And if I've relearned anything about Halton, it's that the Templeworths are absolute sticklers for propriety." They both snorted at that, and he couldn't contain his grin. "So, perhaps your sister will join us tomorrow for a ride on the grounds?"

Francesca narrowed her eyes at him, and he knew even before she opened her mouth that she was going to refuse.

"Well, actually I…"

"She'd love to," Miss Sophia interrupted what was sure to be a rejection, and Adam felt his fondness for the little hoyden grow even more. "Nothing would make her happier."

"Sophia!"

"Goodbye, then," Sophia spoke over whatever Francesca was trying to say, and before he knew it, he was watching their backs as they practically sprinted to the gate leading them home.

It would take an age to understand this afternoon. And copious amounts of brandy. Yet, as he trudged back to the house, Adam couldn't be sorry that he'd kissed Francesca Templeworth. Just as he couldn't wait to do so again.

Chapter Nine

S HE'D BEEN KISSED by Adam Fairchild.
Try as she might, Cheska could not have stopped the words from rattling around her foolish head as she made her way reluctantly to Heywood Manor the next day with Sophia.

She hadn't slept a wink last night, and then she'd endured speculative glances and whispers between Elodie and Hope, who then whispered to their respective husbands, resulting in Christian's announcement that he'd be joining them. Of course, once he'd said that she'd jumped on the chance to cry off. But then a knowing smirk from Elodie and a faux innocent implication of cowardice from Hope and nothing would have kept her away.

She knew they'd done it on purpose. She knew that *they* knew any accusation of being afraid or affected by a man would result in her proving them wrong. But she couldn't help it. She'd rather die than admit the truth—that Adam Fairchild's kiss had shaken the very foundations of her being, and for the first time in her life, she had absolutely no idea how to act around another person.

She wished that she could forget it. Brush it off as a moment of madness. But she couldn't. And it wasn't as though she had no experience with gentlemen. Over the years, she had suitors, during Seasons she'd had to endure the usual fawning, and drivel that came out of their mouths. She'd had her toes trodden on, been simpered at. Yes, she'd run the gamut. Sometimes she'd

Chapter Ten

A DAM HAD NO idea what was happening to him. How he was smiling and laughing and flirting with Francesca Templeworth as though he were happy. As though he were normal.

It baffled him that one slip of a lady could have such an effect on him in such a short space of time. Yet, even though it made no sense, it was true. His dreams, though still plagued with the horrors of war, were sometimes softened by images of Francesca in his arms or by his side.

Sometimes, though, he would find her in the middle of a battle, and try as he might, he couldn't reach her in time. Couldn't stop her from being hurt. Being killed. Those nightmares filled him with such vicious terror that he would jolt awake drenched in sweat and would spend the rest of the night pacing the empty hallways of the house. But they were growing few and far between.

He looked over at her now, his eyes raking over the hair tumbling down her back as they walked their horses at a lazy pace. She was heartachingly beautiful, of that there was no doubt. But what she made him feel? The power she had to make him smile, to make him *live* and not just exist? That went far beyond how she looked. She was the only person who had gotten him to feel something akin to happiness in eight years. Well, she and her madcap family. One of whom had indeed absconded with his horse. And if Brentford weren't with Miss Templeworth, Adam set Cheska's cheeks burning.

"Ah, well, I don't know."

"Come *on*, Christian," Sophia whined as she began the ascent onto Ares with the assistance of a stable lad and a rather high stool. Cheska hadn't realized the animal would be quite so big, but he really was a beast. Surely as big as Valiant, who was snorting impatiently at a safe distance. "If you don't hurry up, I shall tell Elodie you said you're glad of a break from her and the children."

"I did not," Christian said hotly.

"Well, I know that, and you know that. But Elle doesn't," Sophia said with saccharine sweetness.

Christian glared at her but dutifully moved to his own mount. "See?" he called over his shoulder. "A terror."

He didn't await a response, for Sophia spurred Ares into movement with a delighted whoop, and Christian cried foul and shot off after her, leaving a deafening silence in his wake.

"I hope you don't expect me to be able to catch up to them," Cheska said. "Sophia might well have been born in a saddle for all I know. But I most certainly wasn't."

"I was hoping you'd say that," he drawled with a wink before lifting her off her feet and placing her in the saddle.

Francesca was somewhat annoyed with herself that she wasn't annoyed with *him* for manhandling her. But she'd rather enjoyed it. Still, she couldn't let *him* know that.

"Do you think I'm incapable of getting onto my own horse, Lord Heywood?" she asked haughtily.

His smile was pure wickedness.

"I think you would be capable of moving mountains if you wanted to, Miss Templeworth," he answered as he easily climbed into his own saddle, then moved his horse to stand only inches from her own. "But I'll take any excuse to touch you."

Before she could think of a response to that, he took off out into the grounds beyond the stables, and all Francesca could do was follow him.

graveness.

Christian stared at him. Then at Cheska. Then back at him before a smile of his own made an appearance. "Very well, I can see why that was funny," he said, earning himself a slap on the arm.

They hadn't always gotten on as they did now, but Cheska had grown to truly love her sometimes-overbearing brother-in-law. He'd come a long way since his accidental road trip with Elle.

Besides, she'd forgiven Gideon for almost breaking Hope's heart, so she couldn't very well hold a grudge against Christian.

She watched the two gentlemen before her talk about horses and hunting and a plethora of other things she had absolutely no interest in. And as they chatted, she noticed that Adam grew visibly more relaxed, his shoulders not quite as stiff, his countenance not quite as brooding.

"Are you ladies going to stand around gossiping all day or are we riding?"

The gentlemen turned as one to stare down at Sophia, who stood with her arms crossed, one brow raised at them. "This one is a tiny terror," Christian said to Adam by way of an answer.

"I figured as much," came Adam's laughing response. He seemed so relaxed, maybe even happy. And Cheska had the sense that that wasn't something he was used to feeling. Not anymore. "And I don't particularly fancy riling her anymore, so should we go?"

"Ah, you did say I could ride Ares, my lord." Cheska smiled proudly as Sophia switched from irate to innocent, her blue eyes widening imploringly. She'd taught Sophia that particular trick herself. And sure enough…

"Indeed I did, Miss Sophia," Adam said easily. "And I shan't go back on my word. He's spirited though, so…"

"Don't worry," Christian interjected. "I've never seen anyone with a seat as good as Sophia's. And I'll keep pace with her."

"Then I suppose that leaves me to keep pace with Miss Templeworth." Adam flashed her a glance filled with enough heat to heart squeezing as she spotted Adam standing beside Ares, his eyes focused only on her.

Christian and Sophia were already fussing at the horse and laughingly comparing him to Valiant, but Cheska paid them no attention, caught absolutely in Adam's gaze. She could only watch as he ran that gaze over her slowly, as though taking in every detail before his eyes returned to hers.

Lord, she didn't think she'd survive an afternoon of heated glances but, she reasoned, it was as good a way to go as any.

A stablehand rushed over with a stool, but before she'd even handed over the reins, Adam appeared at her side, dismissing the lad with a nod before reaching up, and in one swift movement, lifted her from her mount.

The feel of his hands spanning her waist set off a riot of butterflies in her tummy, and all she could do was tilt her chin and stare at him as he set her on the ground.

"Hello, Sunshine," he said softly.

"My lord." Her voice didn't come out quite as clipped as she'd have liked, and she rather suspected that her face was giving away her inner turmoil given the smirk playing around his mouth.

"My lord?" he repeated with a dangerous glint in his eyes. "Don't you think that's a little formal?"

"It is appropriate," she sniffed, trying to channel some of Elodie's virtue, though she couldn't quite keep her face straight. "And I am nothing if not a model of decorum and propriety."

He stared at her in stunned silence before he burst into a laugh that turned her knees to liquid. She hadn't heard him laugh like that once since he'd come home. Not once. And she was so pleased that she'd managed to get him to do it, that she beamed up at him in response.

"Francesca."

"What's so funny over here?" Christian asked as he suddenly appeared behind Ares, and Adam stepped away, albeit reluctantly.

"Miss Templeworth was just regaling me with tales of her decorum and propriety," Adam said with a mocking sort of she'd let him. Even encouraged him.

She felt that odious heat in her cheeks again and prayed that she would get away with blaming the stiff, autumn breeze.

"Come on," Sophia urged, and without waiting for either of them, she kicked her horse into a canter and dashed across the open meadows toward the manor, with Christian making light work of catching up to her.

Cheska let them go, watching Sophia's dark hair fly out behind her as her breeches-clad legs urged her horse to go faster still. They were always racing when Christian was here. Gideon, too, though he'd stayed behind today to deal with some of Papa's estate business, which suited Francesca quite well since one guard dog was infinitely more tolerable than two.

Neither of them looked back to see where she was. Unlike Sophia, she didn't ride as though she'd been born in a saddle and as though she'd often worn breeches and ridden astride herself. Vanity had taken hold today, and she'd donned her navy-blue riding habit, leaving her hair loose underneath a matching feathered cap. That had earned another smirk from both Elle and Hope before she'd hissed a curse at them and run outside before Mama tried to scold her.

She took off after them at a far more sedate pace, happy to leave seeing Adam again until the last moment—especially since she wanted to stare into those mesmerizing eyes, to inhale his sandalwood and bergamot scent, and to feel those impossibly strong arms pull her closer.

Cheska shook her head, trying to dislodge her wanton thoughts. This simply would not do. She couldn't go in there salivating over the man like some sort of lightskirt. It was embarrassing enough that she'd turned into one of those simpering misses whose entire world revolved around a man. Not that she had, of course. But she was worried that there was a real danger of it.

When she couldn't hold back any longer without seeming as though she'd gone missing, Cheska trotted into the stables, her even like a gentleman, allow him to kiss her hand or ask for a second dance. But never had she felt the way she'd felt in Adam Fairchild's arms yesterday.

She had no idea what to say to him or how to behave. And she hated that. Really, truly hated it. In the normal way of things with gentlemen, she either flirted harmlessly, drank with them shamelessly, pitted her wits against them, or more often than not, cut them down to size with a few sharp words. She couldn't do any of that with Adam. More to the point, she didn't *want* to do any of that with Adam. It was all terribly confusing. And that wasn't even the half of it. There was that tug on her heartstrings she got whenever she saw the world of pain in his eyes. Whenever he looked so bleak that she could almost feel his pain herself.

Well, she needed to rein that in immediately. That's what had gotten her kissed in the first place.

But you enjoyed it.

She would absolutely be ignoring that voice in her head!

"But he can't be *faster* than Valiant," Christian was saying to Sophia just ahead of Cheska. "*As* fast, perhaps. But surely not faster?"

Cheska rolled her eyes, even though Christian couldn't see her. She had no idea whether Christian's horse was faster than Adam's and had less of an idea why it even mattered. Men with their ridiculous competitiveness, she supposed.

Next thing they'd be measuring sword lengths.

They crested a small hill having taken the main road through the village to get here on the horses, and Cheska's heart stuttered as Heywood Manor came into view. It was beautiful but still had an air of abandonment about it. She knew that a skeletal staff had kept the place from falling into complete disrepair, but it was a monstrously big house and a lot of work for a small number of servants.

Perhaps now that Adam was here it would come back to life. Perhaps he would come back to life, too.

Yet, he hadn't felt closed off when he'd been kissing her. And wasn't sure she would bring it back. And damned if he could bring himself to care at that particular moment.

There was a darkness in him still. But she made it a little lighter. A little easier to navigate.

"What are you thinking?" he asked, curiosity getting the better of him. He had wondered if she would be upset that he'd kissed her. Had even considered doing the gentlemanly thing and apologizing. And then he'd decided not to because he wasn't even a little sorry, so there was no point.

She turned to study him, her eyes the color of a summer sky.

"Honestly?" she asked, and he had to laugh.

"I would expect nothing else."

She didn't laugh as he'd expected her to, and his stomach tightened at the serious, hesitant look on her face.

"I was wondering what happened to you," she said quietly. "All these years when we all thought…" She shook her head, as though expelling a particularly grim thought. "We got word that your brother had fallen. But with you? Nothing. And now you're here, but you're so different."

He didn't quite know what to say. How to handle the emotions slamming into him with every word.

"And I know that it was a long time ago, and I was naïve and too young to understand the way of the world, but you were my friend. At least, I hope you were. And I wonder if there's any of that happy man left inside of you. Or if the war and all the tragedies you've faced have buried him forever."

Adam could only stare at her, could only stiffen his shoulders against the storm of feeling and emotion battering against him. His first instinct was to turn and flee. Flee from questions he didn't know how to answer and wishes that he was too afraid to give voice to.

She was astute enough to know that he wasn't that man anymore. Her friend. And too innocent for him to want to tell her why. To destroy all her inherent sunshine and spirit with the bleak reality of war. With the very worst depths of depravity he'd lived through and witnessed.

But he didn't want to run from Francesca. He'd been trying to outrun his demons for years now, and it hadn't worked. He didn't find peace in sleep. Or in solitariness. Or at the bottom of a brandy bottle. Would he find some in honesty with the woman beside him? Did it make him a selfish bastard to find that he *wanted* to share some of this pain, in the hopes that he'd find, deep down, some part of the man he'd been before? Her friend.

He pulled his horse to a sudden stop, waiting for her to follow his lead before dismounting and tossing the reins around the low-hanging branch of a towering oak. He didn't wait for her to attempt her own dismount, instead hurrying to pluck her from the saddle once more. Only this time, he let go immediately, securing her horse and then pacing away into the small woods at the edge of his estate.

He could hear her footsteps hurrying after him and tried desperately to school his features, to not let any of the tumultuous agony hammering at him show on his face before turning to face her.

"I didn't mean to upset you," she said, her tone filled with contrition. But then she tilted her chin as though that innate stubbornness couldn't be smothered for long. "But you did ask, and I checked if you wanted me to be honest."

He was so stunned to be receiving a scolding like a misbehaving boy that it stopped his panicked thoughts in their tracks.

"I know that," he assured her, running a hand through his hair. He hadn't bothered with a hat since none of them seemed to care a jot about appropriate attire. Indeed, the younger one had arrived in breeches and boots! "I've never talked about it before. I've never really been asked about it before, truth be told."

She frowned at that, her brows lowering in confusion.

"Nobody has ever asked you? Not friends? Not anyone?"

"No, spitfire. Perhaps not all of them were as nosy as you," he quipped, or tried to, earning himself a scowl. But his voice was raw, and he knew from her watchful countenance that he was doing a poor job of masking his turmoil.

His sigh felt as though it came from the depths of his soul. He didn't want to tell her any of this, yet conversely, he *did* want to. He had had friends, comrades, and old schoolmates who'd tried to get him to talk. First when he'd been injured and could barely remember his own name. And then when he'd managed to crawl his way back to London.

All of them had backed off after a quick refusal to talk about any of it. And eventually, he'd done such a good job of pushing them away that they'd stopped calling on him. Somehow, he didn't think that would work with Francesca Templeworth. Somehow, he didn't want it to.

"I don't want to taint you with the ugliness of what I went through," he finally admitted. "You are sunshine and light and good. And…"

Her derisive snort interrupted him, and he stared her down as she stepped closer, leaving only inches between them.

"Much as you get great enjoyment from teasing me about my hair, I am very much *not* sunshine and light and all that tosh. That's Elodie. She's the good one."

"She is?" he asked, immediately distracted.

"Absolutely," she said firmly. "Elle is the good one, Hope the flirt. Sophia is the wild one, happier in open spaces with her animals than anywhere near other people."

"And what does that make you then?"

"Nothing good, really." She shrugged. "I am a bluestocking. Too outspoken, too opinionated. Very likely to become an ape-leader with time. And an absolute nuisance to my parents," she finished proudly.

He chuckled softly and couldn't resist reaching out to finger one of the loose curls resting atop her shoulder.

"You're so much more than that, Francesca Templeworth," he said softly. "A nuisance no doubt," he continued, smiling at her growl. "But you are spirited and brave and clever as a whip. Never mind being beautiful enough to make a man weep."

She didn't respond, but her cheeks flushed the most becoming shade of pink that set desire pulsing through his veins.

"And I don't for one second think you'll end up an ape-leader. In fact, I'm shocked that you haven't received at least fifty proposals already."

He'd thought her blush would deepen at his words. Perhaps even expected a coy giggle or a flirtatious bat of lashes. He didn't expect her eyes to narrow so dangerously that he had to fight the urge to back up.

"I have, as it happens," she sniffed. "But when I end up a spinster, Lord Heywood, it will be very much because I want to be one. Why do you assume my being single is the result of the actions of men? Did it not occur to you that I have *chosen* to remain thusly?"

He was in trouble. He didn't quite understand *why*. But he definitely was.

"I just thought…"

"You just thought that a woman couldn't possibly *want* to remain single? You just thought that a woman's only hope for her life is to find a man to purchase her from her father like so much chattel?"

"What? No, of course, not. Don't be so foolish." He'd quite forgotten his distress of moments before in the face of her ridiculous, unjust accusations.

"Don't call me foolish!" she screeched, and he resisted the urge to cover his ears, guessing that it might enrage her further. Christ, but she had a temper. And why the hell did that make his cock twitch?

She stepped closer, her eyes flashing with cobalt fire. "I'll have you know that it *has* been my choice, Adam Fairchild." She poked him in the chest. "So, if you're standing there feeling sorry for the poor, unwanted spinster then…"

"I don't feel sorry for you," he interrupted, his temper rising fully to match her own "I'm *glad* you're not married, you infuriating woman."

Her snort was filled with derision. "Oh really?" she drawled. "And why might that be?"

"Because if you were married, you little hoyden, then I wouldn't be able to do this."

And before she could argue or his own common sense could rear its head, he reached down and kissed her as he'd been dying to do all day.

Chapter Eleven

SOMEWHERE IN THE course of their heated exchange, they'd gotten very much off the topic at hand, but Cheska couldn't bring herself to care as her entire body ignited under Adam's ministrations. She hadn't meant for this to happen. She truly had wanted him to open up about his past. Without quite knowing why, she couldn't help but feel that it was important that he do so. That he ease some of the burden he so clearly held on his shoulders and in his heart.

But his presumptions that she should want to marry, to live some boring, sedate life with a husband had riled her up. She knew most men were taught that way. Most *people* were.

It was getting more and more difficult to think coherently and finally, Cheska just capitulated. Gave herself over to the exquisite feeling of his arms wrapped around her, his tongue dancing with her own. His kiss was drugging, making her feel hot and cold, dizzy, and grounded, here and outside of her body, all at the same time. She moved closer to him.

He reacted to the action as if she'd lit a fuse in him, his hands dropping to cup her bottom and lift her until she could feel the rigid length of him pressed against her center.

When she began struggling to get air into her lungs, he pulled his lips from hers. She opened her eyes to find them caught in the blazing heat of his own.

"You are utterly maddening, Francesca Templeworth. And

utterly irresistible."

She lifted her chin, whether to give him a sharp retort or demand another kiss, Cheska wasn't quite sure. But before she could do either, a fat raindrop landed on her forehead. She looked up just as the heavens opened a deluge of rain that had them soaked in moments. She'd been so caught up in their embrace that she hadn't noticed the clouds darkening the sky.

"Damn it to hell," Adam spat, grabbing her gently but firmly by the arm and pulling her back the way they'd come. "You're going to be soaked through. Come, we need to get back as quickly as possible."

Cheska dutifully hurried after Adam, allowing him to grip her hand as they ran. The sky rumbled ominously, and she knew a thunderstorm was on its way. It was perhaps a little late in the year for one, but it had been warm enough aside from the sharp, cool wind. She didn't mind it.

They reached the horses in seconds, the animals skittish and tossing their heads. "I don't know if I want to risk you riding if she's jumpy," he said of her mare, looking over the beast with an expert eye and grabbing hold of the reins. "But I don't want you walking back through this either."

It was then that Cheska noticed how tight his grip on her hand had become, how stiff his shoulders, the sudden pallor on his face.

"Adam," she said gently. "It's fine. It's just a little storm. I can walk or…"

"No." His voice was as harsh as it had been the first day she'd seen him again, his eyes not deadened but blazing with terror. "No, you'll ride back with me. Come on."

Before she could try to reason with him, he'd lifted her into his arms again and dumped her unceremoniously on top of his horse. And given that she was in a riding habit and his mount obviously didn't have a side saddle, it was precarious, to say the least. Something that he noticed with a blackened oath before she had to point it out to him. Ordinarily, she would have tried to reason with him again or tell him off for being so boorish. But something about him gave her pause. There was something wrong. She didn't know quite what that was, but this reaction to a storm wasn't anything she'd seen before. Even her nieces and nephews never seemed quite so horror-stricken.

And so, when he reached up and abruptly hitched her skirts past her knees, she didn't complain or do anything except allow him to push one of her legs over the other side of the saddle until she was astride. If anyone were to see her, she would be utterly ruined. But she didn't care a whit. Never had done, really. Not about something as silly as that.

Adam wordlessly jumped up behind her, reaching one hand around her waist to grab hold of the reins, the other already reaching out to take control of Cheska's horse. Her heart simply stopped dead in her chest as his body pressed against her own, his hips pushing against her derriere as he kicked the horse into movement. She held herself as still as humanly possible, even as her skin broke out in gooseflesh and her insides turned to liquid.

He didn't speak a word as they made their way back to his stables, their pace hurried. But his breathing was growing harsher. More erratic. And with her back pressed so snugly to his chest, she could feel his crashing heartbeat.

"Adam."

Whatever she had been about to say was interrupted by a boom of thunder overhead followed almost immediately by a flash of lightning. The effect on Adam was instantaneous and alarming. He jumped so much that they almost fell from his horse. As it was the beast reared up in fright and took off at a gallop.

Cheska couldn't contain a scream of fear as she was almost thrown forward. Adam released his hold on the other horse, who immediately bounded off, and grabbed hold of her, wrapping an arm around her waist.

"I have you," he rasped, but his tone was panicked and distant, as if he'd gone somewhere far away in his mind. "I have you."

Francesca knew instinctively that she shouldn't speak, shouldn't make any sudden movements. And so, she sat with her hand gripping the sodden material of his riding jacket and kept her eyes on the stables that had finally come into view. She thought of Sophia and Christian and hoped that they'd either managed to outrun the storm back to the house or had found shelter somewhere. It would likely be the latter since Sophia would have gone miles away on a horse like Ares. And Francesca was fiercely glad she had Christian with her.

They shot into the stables as another rumble of thunder rent the air, the sky flashing in its wake. There were no stablehands around.

Adam threw himself from the saddle, his chest heaving, and Francesca knew that he'd forgotten her entirely when he paced toward the wall and slammed a hand against it. There was nobody around to aide her. Nobody but Adam. And for some reason, he was lost to her right then.

Well, there was nothing else for it, she told herself, willing her frantic heart to calm itself. She was terrified to see Adam in such a state. She had no idea what to do about it. Peering down, she tried to calculate if she'd make the jump off the beast without injuring herself. Probably not, she conceded grimly. Maybe it would be better to get his help, after all.

But before she could call out to him, yet another crack of thunder sounded, this one louder than before, and to Francesca's horror, she could only watch as a pained groan was torn from Adam at the sound, and he dropped to his knees, his hands moving to grip his hair.

"Adam," she cried out in alarm and jumped from the horse.

Her feet slammed to the ground and a sharp, searing pain shot through her ankle as she landed and tumbled forward on her foot. Her eyes smarted with the pain, but that was nothing compared to the pain she felt in her heart watching the man before her fall apart.

It was the storm. It had to be. Her throat hurt from holding back tears as she hobbled toward him, her ankle barely supporting her efforts.

"Adam," she called again, but there was no reaction. It was as though she wasn't even here.

Another clap of thunder and another dry, broken sob from this strong man, prone in front of her, had Francesca throwing herself onto her own knees in answer, her ankle screaming in protest.

"Adam." Her voice was sharpened with fear and pain but he didn't react. And when she leaned forward, she saw nothing in his eyes but wild panic. He stared at her with a frighteningly unseeing gaze before turning away and hunching over so that his palms were flattened against the hay-ridden floor.

She reached out to touch his arm, desperate to offer some sort of comfort to him.

The second her hand made contact with the rock-hard muscle, however, he swung round with a savage snarl, and his hand shot out and connected with her cheekbone. It sent her careening back to the floor.

⋙✕⋘

THE SCREAMS OF *men dying around him were like nails scraping against the inside of his mind as he pushed his way through mud and gore and bodies.*

The tiredness had become so oppressive, the pain so all-consuming, that it took all his efforts to put one foot in front of the other.

Boom. Another gunshot. So close that the spray of blood from its target hit his skin, raining down on him, mixing with the sweat and dirt already coating his skin.

Flash. He was blinded by the light of a musket nearby, the acrid stench of smoke filling his nose and throat.

He had to keep moving. He had to get away. The blood dripped from his head into his eye, blurring his vision and sending him careening to the ground.

No. No! He couldn't get stuck here. He couldn't die on this battlefield. He couldn't leave his father childless. The news had come about Douglas, and Adam had made a promise to the heavens that he'd get himself home.

The noise and light were battering against him with the force of a hurricane. Hands clawed at him. Limbs torn from the bodies of dying men seemed to bury him alive. He couldn't let himself be caught by them. The living or the dead. He couldn't help. He couldn't stop. He couldn't get trapped here.

And then suddenly, another hand, firmer, grabbing hold of him, calling his name.

With a roar of desperation, he batted that hand away. He had to get out. He had to get out.

Chapter Twelve

A DISTINCTLY FEMALE cry rent the air, so out of place in the middle of this hell on earth that it jarred Adam out of his mindless panic. His vision cleared, and he looked around for a second or two, trying to remember where he was. Trying to separate truth from fiction.

He wasn't back there. He was here in England. In Halton. He was safe. It wasn't a battle but the manor house. And the sounds he heard weren't those of war but of a thunderstorm.

He was here and he was with…

Francesca!

He spun around, his eyes frantically searching for her until a groan from the corner caught his attention, and he froze as he saw her slumped on the floor.

"No," he breathed the word as if he could wish away what he was seeing as he scrambled over to her, pulling her back up until she was sitting facing him. He felt his eyes widen in horror as he took in the angry red mark on her face, and his stomach roiled as realization hit.

"No," he whispered again, disgust making him feel like casting up his accounts. Surely he hadn't done that to her? Hurt her like that?

He reached out a shaking hand to touch the angry flesh, and his heart squeezed painfully as she flinched and pulled away from him. Christ, she was afraid. He'd made her afraid of him. The bravest woman he knew, and she was cowering in a corner looking at him as though he were a monster. Because that's what he was. That's what had become of him. And now he'd hurt the only person who'd brought even a flickering of light into the darkness of his world.

"Francesca, I'm sorry. I'm so, *so* sorry."

The fact that he'd scared her absolutely destroyed him, but he couldn't deal with that now, with his demons and with the sickening realization that she'd seen this secret, awful part of him. All of that was secondary to her being hurt at his hands. And he already knew that would haunt him for the rest of his days. That he would never forgive himself for it.

"I won't hurt you," he assured her now, his voice gravelly, barely audible against the rain thrumming on the roof of the stables. Another rumble of thunder sounded, thankfully from further away, but it still didn't stop his muscles from seizing up. It still didn't stop him from having to grit his teeth so hard, he thought his jaw might shatter.

He could get through this by focusing on Francesca. He kept his eyes locked on hers, took steady breaths in and out, in and out. And when he knew he had himself under control again, he lifted a hand toward her reddened face. She'd have a horrendous bruise.

Her wide blue eyes that had been so filled with fear were slowly changing, narrowing, and becoming contemplative as she gazed at him. "Are you well?" she whispered, and he felt another wave of shame crash over him. Was she asking because she was putting his well-being before her own? Or because she was worried that he'd attack her like some sort of damned animal? Probably both.

The laugh that left him was harsh. Brutal. "No. I'm not well," he answered with more stark honesty than he'd shown to anyone in years. "I just hurt you," he swallowed the lump lodged in his throat, willed his heart to slow. "I…" He shook his head, the disgust overwhelming him. "I will *never* forgive myself."

"You know," she interrupted him, her tone bright and casual as though they were two old friends having a friendly chat, and the change was so unexpected that it momentarily snapped Adam from his mawkish apologies. "I've had an unbelievable amount of black eyes and bloody lips over the years."

He could do nothing but gape as she announced this fact proudly. As though it were an everyday occurrence for ladies of Quality to be bloodied and bruised.

"Once when we were girls, Hope got so angry with me for reaching the swing before her that she shoved me off it and then hit me with the wood panel. I had two black eyes and a split lip for *weeks*. So, I cut off a lock of her precious hair and glued it to the top of her lip while she was sleeping so it looked as though she'd grown a curly mustache overnight."

He was rendered completely mute by her tale, by how proud she seemed of it. And a startled laugh was choked from him.

"Of course," she continued in that same, irreverent tone, "nobody has had the injuries Sophia has had. Sometimes I think that girl is more animal than human. She split her head wide open once trying to jump from a tree into the saddle of her horse. We'd seen a similar thing in London when Papa actually remembered we existed and took us to see a trick rider as girls, and she became obsessed with doing it."

Adam's head spun, both from the snippets of her life and the fact that she was chattering about childhood memories after what she'd just seen. What he'd just done. And then, he realized. She was doing it on purpose. Distracting him and talking him down. His heart thrummed with a tenderness that he shied away from. She was hurt, yet she was thinking of them.

"Elodie, of course, never broke or damaged anything. Though I do consider it her fault that I almost choked to death a few years ago drinking brandy and smoking cigars with Christian when he found out he was to be a father. Gideon wasn't around yet, you see. And I really did think I'd be up for the task. The brandy was fine but the cigar?" A shudder wracked her body at the mere memory, and indeed her skin had turned slightly green.

He laughed again, easier this time. He could well imagine this tiny firecracker deciding she could drink and smoke as well as any man.

"Very well," he conceded. "It worked."

"What did?" she blinked innocently when nobody could ever accuse her of being innocent.

Except perhaps in the bedchamber…

Adam put a stop to *those* thoughts before they could go any further. Now was absolutely not the time, and he was surprised he'd even thought it while he was still awash with grief and panic and guilt. But he hadn't lied. Her chattering had worked enough to calm him so he could get them both inside and get a cold compress on that cheek.

His hands were still shaking as he stood to his full height and held one out to her. "Much as I've enjoyed hearing the tales of your exploits, and I truly have, your distractions worked and I'm calmer." The air between them grew thick with silence as they stared at each other. "Thank you," he said softly.

She merely nodded. And he was grateful for that, too. Grateful that she wasn't trying to coax information from him, though she had every right to. Especially since she'd fallen foul of the nightmares that plagued him. And that reminder of her injury was enough to set him moving again, so he reached out and gently pulled her to her feet.

She stumbled and hissed in pain, Adam's arms reaching out to grab hold of her before she fell.

"What is it?" he asked, his panic rising all over again.

"Nothing. I'm fine."

"Tell me what's wrong," he demanded.

She huffed a sigh of frustration. "I just, I twisted my ankle a little when I jumped from the horse."

He frowned before he understood. And that was another load of shame heaped on his shoulders, the weight of it almost buckling his knees.

"It's not your fault," she whispered before he could even say anything. He nodded once. Brusquely. Knew that she was wrong but decided not to argue.

"Let's get you inside," he said in lieu of another sorry that he knew she didn't want to hear. She was cold, wet, and no doubt in a considerable amount of pain. Yet, she'd yapped gaily until he'd come back to himself. He couldn't even begin to explain the magnitude of what that meant to him. "We'll get you dry and seen by a doctor." Before she could object, he bent and swept her into his arms, trying not to notice how perfect she felt there. The rain had done nothing to dull the scent of lemons, and he couldn't stop himself bending to inhale it, letting it fill him and soothe some dark, aching part of his soul. "And then," he continued as he strode toward the house, "you can impress me with those brandy drinking skills."

FRANCESCA WHO HAD always prided herself on being able to lie about doing nothing for hours found that lying about when injured was vastly different and infinitely less relaxing than her usual laziness.

Because this, she concluded two hours later, was excessive. She hadn't been able to move from the chaise since Adam carried her inside, calling orders to his gaping servants as he went. It had taken all Francesca's concentration not to lay her head on his shoulder or reach up to press her lips against his neck.

Her head had been spinning from what had occurred in the stables, her ankle and cheek throbbing. But still, she'd been distracted by the feel of his arms holding her. She'd been fast on her way to tumbling into something dangerously close to love until he'd started clucking over her like a damned mother hen.

First, there had been the poor footman who'd been sent out into the storm, though it had eased a lot by then, to track down both the doctor and her sister and brother-in-law. Then there was the insistence that a bath be run for her in a guest chamber upstairs. A guest chamber that he walked into, ignoring the gasps of shock from the watching staff. And even Francesca, who didn't give a stuff about silly things like appropriate behavior, thought that carrying her into a bedroom in front of people was overdoing it.

Thankfully, Adam had the good sense not to try to remain in the room while she'd bathed and been dressed in a very large, very masculine dressing gown that swamped her and smelled of Adam. She'd been trying to resist sniffing it ever since.

"Well then, Miss Templeworth. That should set you to rights. The ankle is badly sprained, I'm afraid. And you'll need to stay off it for some weeks, then only walk short distances with assistance. I shall leave you with some laudanum to make the pain more bearable."

Francesca was pulled from her wayward thoughts by Dr. Pearse, a handsome if rather bland gentleman who'd come to Halton only a year previously and with whom she'd talked and danced frequently. He was a bit less boring than the other young men of her acquaintance, and so she didn't mind his company too much.

She looked down at him from where he was kneeling and finishing up bandaging her ankle, surprised to see his cheeks a bright scarlet, his brow slightly damp.

"Thank you, Dr. Pearse," she said, smiling at him and trying to ignore the giant hovering over the poor man's shoulder. "Can—"

"What about her face?"

Francesca scowled at Adam, who ignored her completely, keeping his glare trained on poor Dr. Pearse.

"S-she will have some tenderness and bruising for quite a few days, there's nothing for it except ice for the swelling and perhaps some of the laudanum. This was also from your fall off the horse, I presume?"

She watched Adam's face blanch, saw the flinch, and the flash of guilt in his eyes as he opened his mouth to speak.

"Yes," she said loudly. "Yes, that's exactly right. I–I stumbled on my ankle and hit my face off a post. So clumsy of me." She gave him her most charming smile and tried not to wince at the pain of her cheek stretching.

"You are the epitome of grace, Miss Templeworth," Dr. Pearse said, fawning over her as though she were Hope or something. "I'm quite sure that there was no fault on your part."

"Er, thank you," she said, thinking it was doing it a bit brown. "And I shall rest it as much as possible. If Lord Heywood would be so kind as to lend me a carriage, I'm sure that…"

"Ah, I don't think that's the best course of action, Miss Templeworth. Not for a few days at least. The jostling would cause quite severe pain. It would be best if you remained here for a spell. If his lordship has no objection?"

"Of course," Adam said, a look she couldn't decipher in the depths of his emerald eyes. "I will take care of her."

"Perhaps your mama or a sister might be prevailed upon to stay with you, Miss Templeworth. I am aware that even in cases of emergency, your reputation must be protected."

Odious creature! He was just like the rest of the dolts in this town, Francesca thought hotly. And she was ready to offer him a setdown when Adam turned his attention back to the doctor.

"Are you implying, doctor, that the lady's reputation will be in danger while under my roof?"

His tone was so deathly quiet, so filled with rage, that Francesca actually felt a bit sorry for the other man. Indeed, when he started stuttering apologies and assurances that everyone in the room and indeed everyone in a five-mile vicinity was a paragon of excellent behavior and therefore above reproach, Cheska sent a pleading look Adam's way. For his part, he rolled his eyes at her but dutifully set about assuring the doctor that he'd caused no offense and then pushed him toward the door.

"I shall call on you in two days hence, Miss Templeworth. To check on your progress," he called over his shoulder as Adam manhandled him from the room, and then finally there was blissful solitude.

Cheska heaved a sigh as the events of the past couple of hours caught up with her. She couldn't get that haunted look in Adam's eyes out of her mind. It had been the most gut-wrenching thing she'd ever witnessed, seeing him so terrorized by his own mind. And she didn't know how someone like her could help, someone who had no idea of the scars that she suspected were inside rather than without. But she wanted to help. Wanted more than anything never to have to see that look in his eyes again.

She shifted on the chaise, sucking in a breath as her ankle and cheek throbbed. She wasn't usually fond of laudanum, but she would certainly consider taking it tonight if only so she could get some sleep. Sleep here. In a bed here. In Adam's house. Her mouth dried at the idea, and she squirmed again, causing the blanket that had been thrown over her to slip from the chaise onto the Aubusson rug beneath it.

"Damn and blast," she muttered, leaning down to retrieve it and almost tumbling after it.

"What are you doing?"

Looking up, Cheska saw that Adam had returned and was rushing over to her, his face a picture of concern. He still hadn't regained his color, and his eyes were still swimming with shame.

Cheska rolled her eyes, determined to keep things light until they could talk properly about all that had happened. Until Adam felt ready to open up and let her in.

"I'm just picking up the blanket," she muttered, bending to reach for it again.

"Stop!" he shouted. "I'll get it. You are not supposed to move. Didn't you hear the doctor's orders through all the salivating and simpering?"

She looked at him in amazement as he dropped to his knees by her head and pulled the blanket back over her.

"Salivating and simpering?" she repeated.

"Yes," he ground out. "Didn't you notice? I thought being near your bare ankle was going to cause him to have an apoplexy. And then who would treat him? We wouldn't have a doctor," he finished with a grin.

"You're ridiculous," she scolded, but she couldn't help smiling at him.

"No, not ridiculous. Perhaps I'm merely jealous that he got to touch you like that." Her heart came to a complete standstill. And this time when he reached a hand toward her tender cheek, she didn't flinch. She didn't move. She didn't breathe.

There were so many words to say. Too many. They filled the silence between them. But she didn't want to talk right then. And apparently, neither did Adam. For he leaned forward and kissed her.

Chapter Thirteen

He knew he had no right to kiss her like this after what he'd done. But frankly, his emotions had taken such a battering this afternoon that he didn't have the mental energy to keep his defenses up, to resist the ever-present temptation of this fierce, brave woman. A woman who would be staying under his roof. A woman who was in pain because of his actions, his demons. The reminder was enough to cool his ardor, and he pulled back reluctantly, searching her face for signs of pain or tiredness. But he only saw the same desire that he was sure was visible on his own face, and it was all he could do to drop his hand and move away from her.

He cleared his throat, then cleared it again. But his voice still came out hoarse when he spoke. "Are you, do you…"

"What in the hell happened to you?" They both turned toward the door to see Christian and Sophia damp and shivering in the doorway.

Sophia rushed over to Cheska, concerned eyes raking over her, but Christian remained in the doorway, glaring at Adam as though he might wring his neck.

"I fell off a horse when we were running from the storm, Christian," she answered before Adam could say anything. The last thing she wanted was a fight between the two giant men staring each other down. And if Christian found out that Adam had struck her, even accidentally, he'd likely try to put a bullet in him. Then Gideon would take a shot at it. And that would be nothing compared to what her sisters would do.

And until she fully understood his demons herself, she wasn't about to share them with her family. Besides, his secrets weren't hers to tell.

Sophia snorted and raised a brow. "You fell off your docile little horse?" she scoffed. "I managed to get Lord Heywood's beautiful beast back in one piece as soon as the rain let up.,"

"Yes, well, I'm better with people than I am with horses," Cheska groused.

"You hate people," Sophia pointed out.

"I said I was better with them, not that I liked them."

Sophia turned to Adam, her eyes shining. "Oh, he is magnificent, my lord. Truly."

Adam's smile was swift and strained. "He certainly is," he agreed, though his eyes immediately returned to Christian. "Brentford, the doctor suggested that Miss Templeworth remain here for a spell. Perhaps you might join me for a drink, and we can let the sisters catch up." He glanced quickly at Francesca and then away. "He thought that perhaps Miss Sophia might be able to stay, too, for propriety's sake."

"Do you know what's less proper than one single lady under your roof, Heywood?" Christian's voice was deadly quiet. "Two of them."

"It's Halton, Christian, not St. James's. And if you think for one moment I'm spending days alone with my mother for company, you're quite mistaken." He opened his mouth, no doubt to argue, so she continued before he got the chance. "Besides, you and Elle can't drag the children here, and I know neither of you will be without them for long. The same goes for Hope and Gideon. And with Papa still bedridden, there aren't very many options left, are there?"

She smiled sweetly, knowing she'd backed him into the corner.

"Be that as it may, Sophia would actually have to remain in

the house to be any sort of chaperone, and we both know that's not going to happen."

"That's fair," Sophia said unhelpfully.

"I'll be perfectly safe, Christian." Cheska made sure to inject some steel into her voice, and she could tell by the look of defeat in Christian's eyes that he knew she'd outlast him on this.

He looked to Adam, his gaze assessing, his shoulders stiff. "You mentioned a drink?" he asked evenly. Adam merely nodded.

"Lead the way then," Christian said with a long-suffering sigh.

And Francesca knew she'd won this particular battle of wills.

⇛⇚

ADAM COULD ONLY hope that he appeared outwardly calm since his insides were a riot of feelings. He hadn't had a minute to just sit and think since the storm had broken and things had gone so terribly wrong.

And yet, as much as it troubled him to think of hurting Francesca, there was a small part of him that couldn't help but be pleased at the idea of her staying here with him. So different from how he'd felt when he'd first arrived, not wanting anybody near him, not wanting to speak to another soul. Yet here he was, looking forward to a houseguest! But it wasn't just a houseguest. It was his Sunshine. And that was all the difference.

"You do realize that I'll be murdered if I return to tell those women that you're keeping their sisters?"

Adam huffed a laugh as he poured them both a healthy measure of brandy, handing one to Brentford before moving to sit behind his father's desk. Or his desk now, he supposed.

"I am sorry to hear that," he responded smoothly. "But it would be remiss of me not to follow doctor's orders."

Brentford's eyes narrowed, but Adam held his gaze.

"And he ordered her to stay here?"

"He did," Adam assured the other lord. It was the truth, in

any case." "He will call again to check on her recovery and decide if and when she can be moved. But" he added, "it might take some time for her to be comfortable enough for even a short journey."

He knew that the doctor who'd practically swooned when treating Francesca hadn't exactly said that. But he couldn't help feeling that this was an opportunity of sorts. One he shouldn't let pass him by.

He owed her an apology. He owed her far more than that. But it would take time to open up to her. Even then he wasn't sure how to begin doing such a thing. Would it be selfish? To fill her mind with the darkness that he lived with? Darkness he would never want her to know or experience?

"You must be aware that you'll have my odious mother-in-law banging your door down?"

"Better than a father with a weapon, no?" Adam asked.

To his surprise, Brentford's eyes flashed angrily. "In most cases, yes," he answered, his tone suddenly somber. "But even if Templeworth wasn't battling a sickness right now, he wouldn't care that you'd gotten yourself involved with one of his daughters. He probably wouldn't even notice."

Adam felt a spurt of his own anger at that. From the little he'd seen and remembered about the Templeworth sisters, they each had strengths enough to have them lead empires if they chose to. Different strengths, yes, but equal. And it pleased him to think of them, of Francesca, being able to hold their own in a world that so often tried to stop women from doing just that. But it also annoyed him that they had a useless father who wouldn't do that for them.

He thought of the fiery Francesca and the sassy Sophia, the calm and sweet Elodie and the mischievous Hope, and felt a wave of protectiveness wash over him for all the ladies, albeit far more for Francesca. How could a man be blessed with those daughters and not want to give them the sun, moon, and stars? Brentford and Claremont, at least, seemed to truly care for them. And that was a sort of consolation. But with them both living so far from Halton, who did that leave for Francesca and her sister?

"It's a shame they didn't have a brother to look out for them."

Brentford laughed at that. "Don't let Cheska hear you say that. She might be clumsy around a horse, but she's a crack shot and can land a facer as well as any man." He rubbed at his jaw as though remembering being on the receiving end of one of them, and Adam couldn't hide his grin.

"I'd well believe it," he said.

"The girls are each other's fiercest supporters. And Francesca is the fiercest protector of them all."

Adam's heart twisted at those words. Of course she was, he thought to himself. She'd even been protecting him. Hiding the ugly truth about what happened to her this afternoon. And suddenly he just wanted to wrap her in his arms and protect her always. From the world, from uncaring fathers, even from his own demons.

"I'll take care of her here," he promised the other man, sincerity lacing his tone even as his shame threatened to strangle him. Because how could he promise to take care of her, when he was the reason she was hurt in the first place? Would he be so selfish as to allow himself to be closer to her when his demons should mean that he pushed her further away?

Chapter Fourteen

ADAM LEAPT TO his feet as the door to his study burst open, and there was Francesca, chin tilted upward, bedecked in a night-rail that turned almost sheer in the light of the fire. He'd been sitting here wallowing and thinking nothing could distract him from his maudlin thoughts. But this woman, the curves of her body perfectly outlined by the light, her hair a waterfall of sunshine tumbling down her back? That was one hell of a distraction.

Her eyes raked over him and knew that he should put on a jacket, a waistcoat, a cravat. All the trappings of gentlemanly attire that he'd divested himself of the moment he'd locked himself away in here. But he didn't.

He swallowed a sudden lump in his throat, clenching his hands to keep from reaching out to drag her against him. Christ, how had he stayed away from her for these past few days? *Why* had he stayed away from her?

Because you hurt her. Because she deserves more than a terror-filled, broken, shell of a man. Because you could hurt her again.

All true. All things he'd been repeating like a mantra as he lay awake at night thinking of her. Nothing in the world could stem his desire for her. Only the thought of causing her pain kept him from devouring her whole. That's how he'd ended up in here every damned night, pacing the floors, knowing he needed to tell her about the darkness in his heart and terrified of doing so.

"Francesca," he said her name like a prayer. He glanced behind her, expecting to see her sister, but there was nobody there, the house silent save for the crackling of the fire in the hearth. "How did you get down here?" He frowned at the stick in her hand, a reminder of what he'd done. Not that he needed one. He'd thought of little else for days.

"I walked."

"By yourself."

"Obviously."

Her tone was stiff, icy. And it set him on edge.

"Did you need something?" he asked, trying to gauge her odd mood.

"An explanation might be nice," she drawled sarcastically. "Some answers to a few questions wouldn't go amiss."

He bit the inside of his cheek to keep from smiling at the sarcasm. Damn, but he liked this fiery streak in her. Too much. Far, far too much. But he quickly sobered when he realized just what answers she'd be seeking, what explanation she wanted and deserved.

"I know," he said softly. "And I'm sorry for not providing them sooner. It isn't easy for me. I've never told anyone anything about my life since the war."

She stared at him for what felt like eons before she huffed out a breath. "Well, now I feel guilty for asking," she said.

"Don't feel guilty," he said gently. "Trust me, as an expert on the feeling, it's not something I recommend." He heaved a sigh, trying to prepare himself for what was sure to be the most difficult conversation of his miserable life, then held out a hand, stepping forward. "Come, you've told me you have quite the taste for brandy. And you might need a drink because I sure as hell do."

Before she could object, he swept her into his arms, and just like always, his body leapt to attention, fire licking through him, heating the blood in his veins. But *that* was bound to be the furthest thing from her mind and should be the furthest from his, too. So, he kept himself under control and set her gently on the chaise in front of the fire. Wordlessly, he moved to pour her a finger of brandy, refilling his own tumbler while he was at it, before prowling back over to take a seat beside her.

He handed her the glass, which she took with a soft stroke of her fingers that made his chest tighten, and moved it to her lips.

"Wait," he said before she could drink from it. "You didn't take that laudanum, did you?"

She raised a brow at him. "Would I be awake if I had?" she drawled, which he took as an impolite no. She knocked back the contents of her glass, not even flinching as she swallowed, and he felt his jaw drop a little. She'd told him that she could hold her brandy. But seeing it in action was rather impressive. Concerning, but impressive. He went to take her glass to refill it and then thought it would be more efficient to just bring over the half-full decanter.

"You haven't taken it at all?" he asked as he poured her another measure. But she only sipped at that one, demure as though she were having tea with the queen.

"I hate it," she grimaced, then that brow tilted up again. "However, if I'd known I was to be essentially ignored for seven days, I'd have drunk gallons of the stuff. If only to sleep through the boredom."

She had a viper's tongue he decided as her hit landed, and he acknowledged it with a stiff nod. So, there was to be no mindless talk then. Perhaps that was best.

"I'm sorry," he whispered. "About so many things, I hardly know where to start."

She eyed him in silence, and he had the distinct impression she was searching for something. What that might be, he couldn't have said. But he knew she'd been told to go home tomorrow, and he knew that she *would* go home, and he'd miss his chance. And so, he took another steadying breath, downed the contents of his glass, and prepared to open up to someone for the first time since his world had imploded.

Chapter Fifteen

*I*T HAD BEEN bad intelligence. Whether that was on purpose or not, Adam didn't know. All he knew was that he had to get his men out of here. It was a bloodbath; there was no other word for it. They were outmanned, outgunned, outnumbered, and dropping to their deaths in droves.

The screams of his men were torturing him. It was too soon. Only yesterday, he'd been told of Douglas's death. His brave brother who never should have been here. The heir. The one who should have been home safe and making sure the country kept going so the lucky bastards who survived this would have something to go home to. But no, he'd decided to be a hero and fight. And now he was dead. The anger and grief for his brother was like a festering wound, but he had to ignore all of that. He had to make sure he got himself out. His brothers-in-arms out of here.

A shouted French command sounded behind him, and Adam swung round, horrified to see that they'd been circled, penned in like cattle led to slaughter. There was nothing he could do. No way out. They were in the firing line of so many soldiers. Too many. He watched in helpless terror as one by one his men fell. Some screaming. Some with the mercy of silence.

Jefferds, Hackton, Ellis. The men he'd fought with and bled with and even cried with, all staring up at him now with unseeing eyes. And there was young Davy Hubert, who'd grown up in a town not a day's ride from Halton. Barely more than a lad, trying desperately to run for sanctuary when there was none to be found. Davy who'd spoken of how *proud his father would be. Of a girl called Molly, to whom he'd promised himself before he'd come here to make a hero of himself. He'd kept a lock of her hair in his pocket since they'd sailed into battle. And every day since, Adam had seen him toy with the chocolate-brown curl. He could do nothing as Davy ran for trees, hoping to find cover, not realizing that there was no cover to be had.*

None of them would make it out alive. But Davy should. He was barely more than a lad. He had a mother who loved him and a girl who was waiting for him. He had that lock of hair.

So, Adam ran to him. Ran and roared until his throat gave out. And just as he reached him, he saw the flash of light, heard the bang. How that was even possible over the din of battle and dying, he didn't know. But he heard it and he saw it, and he knew they would die.

He only managed to push young Davy into the path of another bullet. And as pain exploded in his skull from the bullet that grazed his head, he felt nothing but failure course through his veins. Jefferds, Hackton, Ellis, Davy. Douglas. And him. What was it for? It seemed so senseless now.

He lay on the sodden ground surrounded by dirt and blood and bodies and thought of a sleepy, English village and a fiery young miss with hair like sunshine. He remembered telling her that war was no great adventure. But he hadn't truly believed it, even as he'd said it. For he had seen it as a grand adventure. And now he would die alone, and his father would have nobody. Nothing. They'd all be forgotten. Wiped from the world as though they'd never existed. And Davy's Molly would wait for a reunion that wouldn't come. Not until she, too, met her maker.

Hours or days or eons later, Adam awoke. His head throbbed, and for a moment, he had no idea where he was. But too quickly, it came roaring back to him. Somehow, the battle was still raging. Somehow, there were enough people still alive to fight.

He lifted his head, wiping at the blood streaming down his face. His mind was sluggish. He was here, and his brother was dead. That much he knew for certain. But where was he? Where was home and how did he get back there? His mind was a pit of confusion, pain, panic, and shame. But by some miracle or curse he was alive. The ringing in his ears was deafening but slowly pieces started to fall back into place. Shattered, scattered pieces, but they were there in the recesses of his mind. Adam. He was Adam. And he needed to get back to England. Back home. And his eyes scanned the sea of bodies, some still, some writhing and sobbing and calling out for a God that he wasn't sure could hear them. But there. Davy. Davy with his eyes wide open and a hole in his stomach. And a lock of chocolate-brown hair in his hand…

"BY SOME MIRACLE, I stayed alive long enough for help to arrive." Adam's voice was hoarse from reliving that last, disastrous day on the front. Everything after that was a blur. He couldn't remember most of it, though he had tried for years. There was the filthy, sweltering tent he'd been patched up in and healed enough to be moved. The trek through towns and villages ravaged by war.

He'd still been making that harrowing journey through the Continent when he'd received the news that his father had died. Just like that, he'd gone from war hero to heir to orphan to marquess. He'd felt it then, the shattering of some final piece of him that thought he might be able to come back from all of this. But he was too broken, too scarred. Too tainted by too many nightmares. Or, at least, he had been until he'd come here to Halton, and Francesca had stormed onto his grounds and demanded to know why he wasn't dead.

Ironic that that conversation had been the one thing to start bringing him back to life when he hadn't thought that was possible.

The silence was excruciating for Adam. He felt hollow and shaken, but strangely, there was a sense of peace, too. Like finally sharing this part of him had eased a fraction of the burden he carried all day, every day. The burden that was his greatest fear. Because, sometimes, he truly did wonder if he'd lost his mind, if he'd end up in an insane asylum, locked up and alone and waiting to die. The mad marquess.

He hadn't shared it to ease his suffering, though. He had

never wanted to sully Francesca's brightness with so much darkness. But he couldn't let her leave tomorrow without knowing. Perhaps she would turn away from him now. Perhaps she would deem him a madman, dangerous, and violent. Perhaps he would never again get to hold her in his arms, or cross mental swords with her, or just bask in the joy that seemed to surround him whenever she was near.

But if that kept her safe from him and from the demons that plagued him still, then he would accept it. Live with it. Live without her.

He was afraid to look up and see disgust or fear on her face. So instead, he stood wordlessly and moved to his desk. Opening the drawer, his fingers trembling like a damned coward, he removed the wax-sealed paper, stained, and wrinkled with age. Untouched save for the times he took it with him on his travels, only to hide it away again. It was time to share another part of the burden. Maybe even let it go.

Letting out a shuddering breath, he walked back toward the chaise on shaking knees and dropped back down beside her. He still couldn't meet her gaze. Not yet. He wasn't ready for this to be the final nail in the coffin of whatever new, delicate thing had been growing inside him and between them.

Hand still trembling, he held the parchment out to her, and when she took it, he noticed that her own hands were trembling, too. In silence, he watched as she broke the seal, the crack of the wax echoing around his skull. In silence, he watched her unfold the paper, then listened to her gasp of recognition as she took in the chocolate-brown curl, tied with a blue ribbon. He'd left the ribbon out of the tale. Had forgotten the color of it even though every other detail was embedded in his mind. He watched as a lone teardrop splashed onto the paper in her hands.

"I took it to try to find her. To-to tell her that she was loved. That he kept her with him until his last, dying breath. But," he swallowed, ashamed of the tears that clogged his throat, "at first, I was too injured. I couldn't remember *why* I'd taken it, only that it was important. And then, then it just, I just…"

He jumped to his feet, suddenly too agitated to sit still.

"I was barely living. I *wasn't* living. Just existing. Drinking and gambling and trying to breathe without the weight of hundreds of deaths on my shoulders. I told myself I'd find her when I got to Spain. Then I told myself it was better to wait until I was back in England. Then, I had to wait until I'd sorted through my father's affairs. Until I'd done my duty to the title as he would have wanted. But those were excuses. And every time I burned through one, I'd just invent another. Because the truth is that I was afraid to face that girl. To tell her that I'd been responsible for bringing her love home alive, and I'd failed. Eventually, I just convinced myself that it didn't matter. She was young. She's probably moved on now and has a husband and children. But she deserves to know."

He finally worked up the courage to look at Francesca. "Those memories haunt my waking hours. The only reprieve I've had from them is you, Francesca. And because of my demons, you were hurt. I didn't think anything could be worse than that war. But what I did to you is worse. So much worse. And I wish to God, you'd never seen me again, for your sake. But I can't be sorry that you came into my life."

Adam's heart cracked all over again at the sight of the tears running down Francesca's face, and he knew then that she would flee. Run from him and the darkness that poisoned his soul. The selfishness that had led to him holding on to that damned lock of hair. The cowardice that had sent him running from his problems.

But when she got to her feet, she didn't move to the door. She wasn't looking at him with fear in her eyes. Pity, yes. Sadness. And a tenderness that made his breath catch.

And before he could think of the words to thank her for not turning away from the demons he carried within him, she launched herself into his arms and pressed her lips against his.

Chapter Sixteen

FRANCESCA'S HEART WAS aching. So much so that she wasn't sure it would ever feel light again. She couldn't think of a single thing to say that could ease the sorrow in Adam's eyes. She couldn't think of a way to tell him that what he'd gone through and what he still had to shoulder didn't make him bad or insane or any of those horrid things he thought about himself. To tell him that she didn't fear him. And would never fear him. That he had a journey of healing to go on and that he hadn't yet started.

She trusted him implicitly and knew he would never, ever purposefully harm her. And that if he would allow her to, she would take every step of that journey with him. It was too soon, far too soon for her to be thinking that way and feeling what she felt for him. Another thing she didn't quite know how to describe. But she felt it anyway. Keenly and deeply.

And so, she did the only thing she could think of to even try to communicate the tumultuous emotions raging through her. She kissed him.

Francesca felt Adam's shoulders stiffen under her touch and for one, awful moment, she thought that he would push her away. But then, with a groan of capitulation, he wrapped his arms around her and pulled her closer until every inch of her was aligned with the heated hardness of his body. It was only when she felt what thin barriers both of their clothing provided that she realized she'd come to him in nothing but a thin cotton night rail, her hair tumbling down her back in a mess of curls.

Francesca was able to feel just how deliciously solid his body was, feel the ridges of his tightly packed muscle, and feel the thunderous racing of his heart, which surely echoed her own.

The kiss had been meant as a comfort, a testament to how much she admired him for fighting every day against such unspeakable horrors, how much she trusted him. But the second Adam took control of it, she was lost. The fire that always seemed to crackle just beneath the surface of her skin when he was around, exploded into a leaping flame that incinerated the world around her so there was only him, only the feel of his tongue and his hands.

He dragged his mouth from her own to bury his face in her neck, breathing her in, nipping at her earlobe until she was trembling from the strength of the desire he awoke in her.

"Adam," she rasped. A question or a prayer or an answer. She didn't know which. But it was enough to spur him on. Enough so that his hands moved to her neck, tilting her head just so, and he kissed her again with a passion that nearly melted her into a puddle at his feet.

She didn't know if talking had unleashed something in him, but it certainly felt like it. There was a wildness to him as he tasted her again and again. A desperation that she didn't quite understand, but that she relished, nonetheless. He pulled her closer, and she stumbled a little on her injured ankle.

He froze. "I'm sorry," he whispered against her lips, his tone an agony of regret and desire. "I don't want to frighten you. To hurt you."

Francesca pulled her head back, causing him to drop his hands as he stared at her, hands clenched at his sides, chest heaving as he struggled to breathe. She knew the feeling.

Slowly, she lifted her hands to his face, holding him still so that he had to look straight into her eyes. So he could read the depth of sincerity in them. "You won't hurt me," she said. "I see you, Adam Fairchild. Every scar. Every nightmare. I see all of you, broken and healed, and I am not afraid."

His eyes lit with unholy fire, and she could tell that whatever thread of control he'd been clinging to snapped. He pounced on her again, lifting her off her injured foot and carrying her to the giant, mahogany desk by the chaise, all while plundering her mouth.

Cheska's legs parted on instinct, and she couldn't stifle her needy moan as she felt the solid length of him pressed against her pulsing core. His hands moved over her hips, cupping her, and dragging her closer to the edge of the desk and to the edge of sanity.

Pulling back, he stared at her, something like wonder mixed with the unadulterated lust stamped on his beautiful face.

"I'm not going to ruin you on a desk," he growled, but it sounded more as though he were telling himself that than her.

"Why not?" she panted, and his answering laugh was gruff, even a little desperate.

The question surprised her and yet didn't. She'd often walked the line of propriety, but never crossed it. Yet with him, even if it made her a lightskirt, a disgusting wanton, she didn't just want to cross it, she wanted to obliterate it.

"Because you deserve more, so much more than that, Sunshine," he said, running his knuckles along her heated cheek. "I won't take your choices from you, no matter how much I might want to."

"They are *my* choices," she said, wondering if she sounded as though she were begging and wondering if she even cared. The need that had awoken in her was torturous, and she knew only he could ease it. Only he could give her what her body was aching for. "And frankly, you've started something now that you'd better bloody well finish."

He tilted his head back and laughed, the sound deep and guttural, and it sent a shock of pleasure right to her core.

"You are a hellion, Francesca Templeworth. A beautiful, irresistible hellion."

"Hmm. So I've been told." She shrugged, marveling at the fact that she could joke with him when he was standing between her legs, and she was almost perishing from need. And then suddenly, an awful, humiliating thought hit her. "D-do you not want…?"

She couldn't bring herself to finish the question, and she looked down, starting to feel foolish and unsophisticated and more than a little embarrassed. But his fingers were under her chin in seconds, tilting her head up, and she gasped as his other hand grabbed hers and brought it flush against him.

"Does this feel like I don't want to?" he asked through clenched teeth, and for one of the very few times in her life, she was completely lost, so she shook her head, not trusting her ability to speak at that moment.

"You deserve so much more than me, Cheska," he said. "So much better."

"I don't want more," she insisted. "Nobody has ever made me feel like you do. I feel as though my blood is on fire. I feel as though I might explode if I don't, if you don't…"

She didn't have the words to convey her feelings. But as it turned out, words weren't necessary, for with a muffled oath, he kissed her again.

THIS WOMAN. THIS brave, beautiful, incredible woman. She would be the death of him. Adam struggled more than he would have thought possible to hang onto that tiny modicum of sense and decency as he once more captured Francesca's mouth with his own.

I see all of you, broken and healed, and I am not afraid.

Never would he have thought he'd be lucky enough to hear those words. Especially not from someone who had the power to turn his world on its head. Who could so easily destroy him but chose instead to save him? From his own mind and from a desolate future, void of any light. Because he knew with certainty that he would never find anyone like Francesca Templeworth, and he would never want anyone as much as he wanted her.

He ran his mouth down her throat, stopping to lick the frantic pulse at the base, and laughing softly against her skin as her breathing hitched and her hips surged against his straining cock.

Christ, she was responsive. He'd give anything to just free himself and plunge into the depths of her, taking her for his own, ruining her for anyone else. But the only thing stronger than his desire for her right then was his affection for her. And regardless of her painfully compelling arguments, her first time wasn't going to be on a damned desk. It wasn't. He-he couldn't.

But she felt so good, and she tasted like ambrosia, and he couldn't resist feeling more, tasting more, craving more. He moved his hands, smoothing them over the curves he could feel through the thin material of her nightgown, back over her hips to cup the delicate mounds of her breasts, flicking his thumbs over the stiffened peaks, delighting in her moans and sobs and breathless little cries that set the blood boiling within his veins.

It wasn't enough, it was nowhere near enough. With a growl of frustration, he grabbed hold of the loose strings holding the front of the material together and made light work of loosening them enough to shove the garment off her shoulders, freeing her naked flesh to his greedy eyes.

"You are so beautiful," he rasped before leaning over her and pushing her back against the desk. And in that moment, he knew what it was that he'd been feeling for her these past weeks. Knew why he'd been slowly feeling as though he could find true happiness again. Maybe even for the first time ever.

"So are you. But still terribly masculine, don't worry," she gasped with a small, breathless laugh, and he could only smile at that honesty again. At least he knew that she would always tell him exactly what she was feeling. But he didn't need words to know what she was feeling then. The lust was stamped across her face as surely as it was stamped across his own.

Adam leaned over, placing his hands on either side of her and bending to kiss her jaw, her throat, and lower until he reached her breast and pulled one nipple into his mouth, sucking and biting and teasing until she was writhing beneath him, before moving on to give the same attention to the other.

He moved his hand to grip the material of her nightgown, bunching and slowly pulling it up, inch by inch, until the material gathered at her waist. He tugged his mouth from her to look down, groaning at the perfection of the body exposed to him. Once again, that urge to claim her fully roared inside him, stronger than before. But he couldn't. Not until he knew for sure that he could be worthy of her. That she would be safe with him. And safe *from* him.

For now, though, he could give her enough pleasure to know how he wished to worship her. And to know how much he wanted her. He dropped to his knees before her, pulling her closer to the edge of the desk, and she gasped as she shot up on her elbows.

"What are you doing?" she hissed, her hair tumbling around her in waves of gold.

He lifted her good leg onto one shoulder, her damaged one even more carefully over the other, all the while keeping his eyes locked on hers. And then he smiled, the expression widening as he felt her toes curl against his muscles.

"You said you trusted me," he said gruffly.

"I do." Her answer was immediate and a balm to his weary soul.

And he responded by bending his head and finally tasting her, laughing softly against her as she lay back and swore like a particularly imaginative sailor. But the words became deliciously incoherent sounds fairly quickly. And when the sounds then became pleas interspersed with his name, he knew she was on the edge of release. So, he slipped a finger inside her, moaning right along with her at the tight, hot heat he found within, and when she exploded on his tongue and hand, crying out into the still, night air, something primal and possessive awoke inside of him and settled right into his heart.

Chapter Seventeen

"I AM SO sorry to hear that the pain has worsened, Miss Templeworth. It is rather concerning since the swelling has been reduced. Perhaps we should attempt to have you removed to your home. I'm sure being around your family and the servants who know you will help in your recovery."

Francesca tried to keep her expression calm and hoped that her cheeks weren't as scarlet as they felt. Sophia was frowning at her in confusion, and Adam, well she was avoiding looking at him because one glance at that male smugness that was radiating from him and she'd give herself away.

"Oh, I…"

"I don't think we should make any rash decisions," Sophia suddenly interjected, and Cheska turned suspicious eyes on her. Close as they were as sisters, there was no possible way that Sophia could know Cheska was just trying to prolong her stay here. "If my sister feels that she should rest here for a little longer, then perhaps that's what's best."

"Well, I…"

"And, of course, I shall stay with her for as long as she needs. Weeks even, if that's what it takes."

"Oh, that won't be necessary."

"After all," Sophia continued, doing it all a bit brown, "I have a very giving nature, and nothing is more important to me than the horse."

There was a moment of complete silence before Sophia's eyes widened. "My sister! I meant my sister." She thrilled a laugh. "I don't know where that slipped from."

Francesca rolled her eyes. Sophia's claims that she was only looking out for her sister's welfare were a little hard to believe considering she was literally sitting in riding gear and was practically chomping at the bit to get back outside. Not that Cheska really minded that. There were only weeks left of the autumn, and though Sophia rode through the winter, too, it wasn't always as easy for her to do so. And Cheska knew she hated being cooped up inside. Plus, there was the small matter of wanting desperately to be alone with Adam.

Her eyes flew to him of their own volition, and she found his gaze locked on her, a tiny smile playing around his mouth. The mouth that she knew now could do unspeakably wicked, delicious things. The mouth that just last night had spent hours teasing and tasting and…

"Miss Templeworth, you are extremely flushed. I do hope you're not running a fever."

Francesca's mind snapped back to the present just as Dr. Pearse leaned over to press a hand to her forehead. She blinked rapidly a few times, trying to drag her wanton thoughts out of her mind. A quick glance told her that Adam's smile was now a fully-fledged, self-satisfied grin. One which she pointedly ignored. Just as she ignored the soft chuckle when she sniffed piously and looked away. The doctor was still fussing at her, so she batted his hand away. "I'm fine," she snapped, her patience wearing thin. "I just tired. I–I didn't get much sleep last night."

A cough from the doorway where Adam stood had her clenching her teeth. Arrogant creature. She had a good mind to pack up her belongings and her sister and go home. She might even let Sophia steal his horse after all.

Only, she didn't want to leave him. Ever, she was coming to realize. Just as she was coming to realize what she'd done. What she'd allowed herself to fall into. Romantic tosh that she'd usually roll her eyes at, that's what.

Yet, she felt it keenly. Especially after last night. Not just the pleasure he'd rung from her body, and the way he'd guided her to do the same for him. Not just the hours they'd spent talking, long, long into the night until the sky began to brighten. How he'd told her more of his past. How he'd trusted her enough to tell her of his nightmares and about the things that sometimes made him think he was back there. Made him think it so much that he couldn't tell what was real and what wasn't.

And when she hadn't been able to stifle her yawns any longer, the way he'd swept her into his arms, holding her as though she were the finest, most precious thing in the world, and carried her to her bed, laying her down, kissing her gently on the forehead and then staying beside her while she drifted off to sleep.

It had been only hours later that the maid he'd assigned to take care of her bustled in. And when Francesca's head snapped around to the pillow beside her, she saw that he'd left before anyone could discover them. But his scent had lingered and driven her mad until Sophia had barged in and demanded that they eat so she could go riding.

"If that is suitable, Miss Templeworth?"

Francesca noticed that Dr. Pearse was staring at her expectantly, and she realized that once again she hadn't been listening to a word the poor man was saying. "Oh, er." She hesitated, trying to guess at what the right answer would be. But before she took a stab at it, Adam pushed off the doorframe he'd been leaning against and stepped forward.

"I'm sure Miss Templeworth understands your need to be out of town for a few nights, Pearse. Don't worry, I shall take excellent care of her."

Francesca resisted the urge to fan herself at the heat in Adam's eyes as they alighted on her once more. His wink was so subtle, she was quite sure nobody else had noticed it, and she smiled conspiratorially at him before bidding farewell to Dr. Pearse and shouting goodbye to Sophia's back as her sister raced from the room, leaving Adam and Francesca quite alone.

"Can I get you anything?" Adam prowled closer, and Francesca felt her heartbeat kick up a beat or two. Even the way he *walked* was attractive to her, for goodness' sake. She probably wasn't going to survive these next few days with him.

"No, thank you," she said, her voice coming out squeakier than she would have liked.

It was just that in the cold light of the brisk autumn day, it was a lot easier to remember that young, single women weren't supposed to throw themselves at young single men and make love to them in the small hours. And while Adam had insisted that they not go past the point of no return, they'd certainly done enough to ensure she couldn't be considered entirely innocent anymore.

And it wasn't that she hadn't enjoyed it, because it had been the greatest night of her life. It was just the terrible inconvenience of having fallen head over heels in love with him and having no idea what to do with herself around him now.

"You did say that you struggled to sleep last night. Or perhaps I should say this morning." His grin was positively wolfish. "So perhaps a cup of tea. Coffee even?"

"No," she repeated more firmly. "Thank you."

"Very well." He sat on the chaise beside her, jostling her enough that she scowled at him but couldn't do much since her bad ankle was still propped on the ottoman Dr. Pearse had used while examining her. "How about I just kiss you senseless instead then?"

He said it so casually that it took a moment for the words to sink in, and she found herself lifted bodily and placed on his lap. "I..." She didn't even get a word out before his lips were on her own, devouring her as though he were a starved man and she the most delicious meal. It was intoxicating, addictive, everything she wanted and needed, and she wrapped her arms around his neck, giving herself over entirely to the maelstrom of feelings he awoke in her.

But all too soon he pulled away, panting slightly as he laid his forehead against her own. "You'd drive a saint to sin, Francesca Templeworth," he whispered, his voice coarsened with longing. "But even I think putting on a show for the staff might be a bit much. So instead, why don't I take you on a drive around the gardens."

The world of promise in his eyes was far too tempting to resist, and it was all Francesca could do to nod her consent, not trusting herself to speak.

"I'll be back," he promised with a swift kiss to her forehead before he lifted her from his lap back onto her seat and darted from the room.

He looked younger, Cheska mused as she sat and waited impatiently for him to return and take her away so they could be alone. More at ease. More at peace. He bounded back in, his eyes lit with something she hadn't seen in them before. Something tender and joyful. And as he carried her outside to his gig, even though she'd argued that she could hobble along without him, she realized what that light was. He looked happy.

ADAM RAN AN eye over the gardens and grounds as they passed by in the gig. He'd brought pillows for Cheska's foot and had wrapped her in a blanket large enough for her to drown in before he'd been satisfied that she wouldn't get cold.

Only days ago, he'd sat down with the head gardener and instructed the man to hire more workers for the estate. Then he'd instructed both the housekeeper and the butler to do the same for inside. He didn't care how many they needed. He just wanted to make sure he had a full staff to run the house.

They had complied straight away, but he hadn't missed the speculative glances they'd shared. For years, he'd left the manor house in the care of a skeletal staff. And when he'd first arrived here, he hadn't bothered hiring more. But over the last few days, he'd decided that he wanted to make the place nice again. Father had always loved it here. And if Adam got his way, he'd likely be spending a lot more time here in the future. So, he wanted to make sure it was brought back to life. Just as he was being brought back to life.

Most of the work outside of the formal gardens was clearing years of neglect and growth, he knew. And indeed, there were small, controlled fires lighting as far as he could see over the vast property.

The air was cool and crisp, filled with the scent of burning wood, and the trees were a riot of golds and reds. It was a beautiful afternoon. One he actually thought he could manage to enjoy. Thanks in no small part to the woman beside him.

He glanced over at her to see her face tilted toward the weak autumn sun, a smile playing around that mouth. The mouth that had done such incredible things that he was growing hard just remembering it. Damn, but she was a fast learner, he thought as he gripped the reins on the matching pair a little tighter. Enthusiastic, too. And the sounds she made… Adam shifted uncomfortably in his seat. He was no better than a green lad with his wayward thoughts.

It was just that last night had been, in a word, spectacular. A night filled with so much emotion that it had burned him to ash. So much passion that he'd been forged in the flame of it and made anew. He had a long way to go before he could consider himself healed. And truthfully, he suspected, he never truly would be. Not fully.

The scar on his temple might fade over time. But the ones inside would remain. Yet, he did not fear them, as he once had. He did not shy away from them. And, this was the most shocking thing of all, he wasn't as ashamed of them as he had been.

"It's so beautiful at this time of year," Francesca interrupted his musings, turning to smile at him, her eyes made bluer by the low sun behind her, her plum-colored spencer the perfect foil for her golden hair and creamy skin.

Behind her stretched acre after acre of fields already being harvested by his tenants. Tenants, he realized, that he hadn't even bothered visiting since he'd arrived. "It's my favorite time. Do you remember the harvest festival your father used to host? I know they only happened when I was a girl, after that you usually only visited at Christmastide. But I'll never forget those festivals. The music and dancing. Everyone all together, servants and merchants and everything."

He smiled indulgently at her thinking if that was all it took to get that light shining in her eyes, he'd host a month-long harvest festival every year. And he realized with a jolt that he actually meant it. "I do remember," he said while his mind churned with ideas and hastily made plans. "The cider and spiced beef."

"Yes," she cried giddily. "And the bonfire so big, I thought it would surely reach the sky," she continued with a laugh. "Apple pies and plum pudding. Oh, it was divine." Her wistful smile twisted his heart. For someone who claimed to be a cynic, she certainly had a romantic streak. And one that he would happily indulge.

"Well then, perhaps it's time to bring it back."

Her eyes snapped to his, sparking with excitement. "Truly?" she asked. And he laughed as he nodded. "Truly. Why not? It might not be a grand affair. At least not until next year. Until we have longer to plan it. But I'm sure if I put you at the helm even a couple of weeks will be long enough to put together a diverting event."

"Me?" she asked a little breathlessly.

"You," he said firmly. "It's your idea. Your favorite time of year. And I wouldn't do it for anybody else."

She smiled softly at that, her cheeks turning a delicious shade of pink. And the words built up inside him, wanting so much to burst forth that he had to think of something to say to distract them both.

"Besides, since half the village is in love with you and your sisters, and the other half of terrified of you, I don't think anyone else would be quite able to pull it off."

She gasped in mock outrage and slapped his arm, and they drove around for hours, playfully arguing about which of them was more terrifying to the locals and making plans for the party he was not only willing to throw but was rather looking forward to.

Chapter Eighteen

"THE CHILDREN MISS you. And Nell is already bigger. I swear I've never known an ankle to take so long to heal." Francesca held Hope's eye over the oak table in Adam's large dining room, refusing to look elsewhere, even though she suspected her sister was seeing far too much in her face.

"Well, it was a very bad sprain," she said calmly, scowling slightly as Hope grinned mischievously. Beside Hope, Gideon was glaring daggers at Adam, and further down the table, Christian was doing the same. Thankfully, Adam didn't notice because Mama had been commanding his attention for the entire dinner.

She and Sophia were returning home tomorrow because even they had to acknowledge that they'd stayed too long. It had been almost two weeks now, and though they'd been the happiest of Francesca's life, she knew that she'd pushed her boundaries to their limit. And her brothers-in-law to their limit, too. Adam had decided to invite her family to dine as something of a farewell.

Stifling a sigh, she turned to Elodie, hoping that her older sister would play the part of peacekeeper as she always did. "Elle, will you be able to stay long enough for Ad-er, Lord Heywood's harvest festival?"

Elodie's eyes narrowed shrewdly at Cheska's slip, but she merely smiled, smoothly reaching out to release Christian's white-knuckled grip on his knife before answering. "Yes, I hope so. The children will enjoy it, and since Papa is still not on his feet, I think our stay may be extended a little longer."

The reminder of their father's ill health seemed to settle on all of them. He hadn't been a particularly kind or good father. But he was still their father. And it was odd to think of him missing from their lives.

"And is Dr. Pearse still calling on him daily?" Cheska asked.

"Yes." The answer unexpectedly came from Gideon, whose dark eyes bored into her. "An odious creature, but he knows what he's doing. Except when it comes to ankles, it seems."

Once again, Cheska found herself holding that stare and praying that her face gave nothing away.

Gideon glanced to Adam, who was no longer even pretending to listen to Mama's whittering and was instead staring at Gideon. "He'll be happy to have you back at the house, Cheska," Gideon continued smoothly. "He speaks very highly of you. I think he might have developed something of a *tendre* for you."

"Yes, or your ankles in any case," Hope added with a wink.

The table rattled suddenly, and she looked up to see that Adam had thumped his wineglass down so hard that the claret spilled all over the white linen.

"Forgive me," he said to nobody in particular, his tone carefully flat.

Francesca glared at Gideon, who was looking as though he'd discovered the answer to some unspoken question. And she knew, she just knew they were going to try to cause trouble. That they already *were* trying to cause trouble.

"Yes, well, I have rather nice ankles, so I don't blame him," she said with a shrug, earning a reprimand from their mother and a tsk from Elodie.

"You do have nice ankles," Sophia spoke up in support. "But I still don't understand how you wrecked one of them getting off that tiny horse."

Francesca's eyes flew to Adam at Sophia's comment. She was

sure that it would set something off in him, something dark and pained. Though he grimaced, he offered her a smile. And she was able to huff out a sigh of relief.

She could read him so well now. She knew that the guilt still hung over him. Not just for hurting her but for young Davy and his Molly. For the men he'd lost. For that lock of hair tied up in a blue bow.

He didn't want her to leave, she knew. He'd whispered as much to her last night before he'd crept from her bedchamber. He'd taken to sneaking in and out like a thief in the night. And sometimes she wondered if he didn't want to get caught and stuck with her forever. But then he would kiss her the way he did and touch her the way he did, and she simply couldn't believe that he would do that and not feel *something* for her.

Perhaps not the all-consuming love she'd been afflicted with. But *something*. Enough that she still found herself having to reassure him that she wasn't in pain any longer.

"I told you. It was wet, the horse was spooked. Just one of those things. And," she continued loudly when it looked as though Sophia might speak again, "if Dr. Pearse has the good sense to be enamored of my ankles, then that's very flattering, but I have absolutely no interest in the doctor."

"Of course, you don't," Sophia scoffed. "Lord, he's almost as bad as Elle's pig farmer." The sisters burst into peals of laughter and began to regale Adam with tales of Elodie's almost-engagement to Christian's cousin, which led to a discussion about Gideon's almost having a secret baby with his own stepmother.

"It sounds worse than it is," Hope protested loudly, and as they sat there laughing and poking fun at matters that at the time had been really quite traumatic, she realized that Adam's attention had remained fixed on her.

"So, not all of you had smooth beginnings then?" he asked of the spouses at the table.

"No, Lord Heywood. Sadly, my sister and I managed to fall in love with two of the most obtuse men in the country," Elodie laughed.

And that set off another boisterous argument about whose fault those rocky starts had been. The sisters, of course, blamed the two lords. And the men defended themselves by asking who *wouldn't* find it difficult to navigate their way through a tussle with the Templeworth girls.

"But when all is said and done," Christian spoke when the furor had died down, his eyes glowing as they looked at Elle, his face a picture of adoration, "it was worth taking my life into my hands with these girls if the prize was my beautiful wife."

"Here, here," Gideon said, taking Hope's hand and pressing a kiss on it while giving her a roguish wink. "And I think perhaps that bumpy road made it so much better when we finally found our way. I can appreciate how lucky I am when I know I had to fight to get here."

To Cheska's horror, she felt her eyes fill with tears at the words of both these men whom she hadn't trusted an iota at first, but who had earned her sisters' love. And her own, too, over time. She had entrusted her sisters to them, and no two men could have been a better match for Elodie and Hope. Funny that she hadn't reserved that cynicism for Adam.

From the moment she'd found out he was still alive and back, she had trusted him implicitly. Had felt safe around him, even after that awful incident in the stables. She looked up at him again to find him smiling at her, such tenderness in his eyes that her breath caught. And she didn't know what that look meant. She only knew what she wished with all her heart it might mean.

ADAM HEAVED A sigh as he rested his head against the back of his chair. This evening had been eventful. But fun. He'd enjoyed his time with Cheska's family. Except for her mother, who took every possible opportunity to berate one of her girls. He'd wondered if perhaps he was misreading the shrill woman, but then he'd noticed the irritation and carefully banked anger on Brentford and Claremont's faces and knew that he wasn't imagining it at all.

It was clearly something they all just put up with. And the girls, to their credit, paid no attention to it. Still, it bothered him to see anyone make a disparaging comment about Francesca.

He'd suffered through a bit of a setdown from the two lords when the ladies retired to the drawing room, giving them the bare details of his time in the army and his various holdings. But after a few tense moments, they'd both relaxed with him. And he couldn't be angry that they were protective. He would be the same. He *was* the same.

In fact, when Claremont had casually suggested that the girls leave with them tonight after dinner, he'd had to physically restrain himself from grabbing hold of Francesca and gluing her to his side. Thankfully, Sophia had objected quite ferociously to missing out on one last morning with Ares, and the earl had had the good sense to back down. He'd been so grateful to the little hellion that he'd almost been tempted to give her the horse.

He was waiting to make sure that the entire household slept before creeping upstairs. But tonight, he wasn't sure if he wanted to go to Francesca. No, that wasn't true. His blood sang to go to her, his heart thrummed for her. But tonight was to be their last night together until he got some things in order. And even though she was only going back to the other side of the village, it still felt like something was being taken from him. Something so precious, he was terrified of letting it go. He didn't know if he could hold onto his resolve. Which was why he was sitting here in the dark, missing her with only feet between them.

But, he reassured himself, she'd be here almost every day to oversee the festival that he'd rightly predicted she would run with an iron will and frightening efficiency. They could have done with her in the war, he mused. She'd have been a general in no time.

Perhaps he should have let her help with the letter he'd penned. The letter it had taken him eight years to write.

Adam heard the creak of the floorboard and knew without turning that she'd come to him again. Like that first night that had changed everything for him. For them. He lifted his head in time to see her glaring down at him, one brow raised, and his blood heated immediately.

He loved it when she was soft and giving, when she pleaded for him to take the edge of her need. But he also loved it when she was fiery and sassy, and he had to kiss all that rage out of her. Sunshine with a mean streak. And clearly, he'd annoyed her.

"What are you about, making me come looking for you in the middle of the night and on a bad ankle?" she demanded before he got the chance to ask what he'd done. He felt a smile tug at his lips.

"Forgive me, Sunshine." He bowed his head. "I got caught up in thinking." He was watching her so closely that he saw her start a little.

"Are you well?" she asked, unusually hesitant, and he knew that she was thinking of the episodes he'd told her about.

"I'm fine," he told her, not quite honestly. "I was just thinking about how much I'm going to miss having you around me." He paused, then grinned wickedly. "And under me." Her breath caught in that way that drove him wild. But she tilted her chin, even as he stood and began to prowl toward her, refusing to back down.

"Well, you have a funny way of showing it," she sniffed. "Ignoring me."

"Missed me, did you?" He grinned again, and she practically hissed in response. But then her eyes cleared, and she shrugged her shoulders, making to step around him. Barely limping now on her "injured" ankle.

"Maybe a little," she said nonchalantly. "But I would never want to impose on all that thinking you're doing. I'll bid you goodnight." She moved toward the door, tossing words over her shoulder. "I happen to know of a gentleman who seems quite taken with me. And my ankles. So, if you can't…"

He didn't give her the chance to finish that sentence, growling as he grabbed hold of her arm and spun her back to face him. Pressing his mouth to hers, he wasted no time in nipping at her bottom lip and taking the opportunity of her gasp to deepen the kiss while he bent and lifted her.

"You don't need to carry me anymore," she pulled away to tell him, her eyes bright, her breathing shallow. "I'm perfectly capable of walking."

"I want to carry you," he said gruffly, and when she opened that mouth of hers to argue, he leaned down and kissed her again. "I want to take every opportunity to hold you for as long as I can," he whispered against her lips.

She rolled her eyes but snaked her arms around his neck. "Fine," she said in a long-suffering tone. "I suppose I should take care of my ankles anyway. Since they have such an admirer."

"I'm going to make you pay for that," he warned her as he hurried toward her bedchamber and the ecstasy he knew awaited him there.

Chapter Nineteen

Francesca's heart was beating so fast, she was afraid it would burst from her chest and take flight. She was a bundle of nerves, excitement, and everything in between. She'd lain awake waiting impatiently for Adam to appear as the household quietly settled down to sleep. Would he yield to her on this, she wondered as she lay there counting the seconds?

Would they take that final step? The one from which there was no going back? She had turned over yet again to check the time, and when she saw that the usual hour in which he came to her had passed, she had worried that something was wrong and that he needed her.

It was that worry that had her throwing off the coverlet and hurrying down to the study as fast as she could.

Adam made light work of the stairs, and in only seconds, they were in her bedchamber. Not hers, she reminded herself with a pang. This wasn't her room. Her home. Even if it had begun to feel like it. Adam set her on her feet and kept his eyes trained on her as he reached behind him and locked the door. The click seemed to reverberate around the room, and a shiver of anticipation coursed through her.

"I'm going to miss having you here every day," he said softly. She could only watch as he prowled closer, a hunter with an eye on his prey. "I'm going to miss your scent floating around the house, driving me to distraction. I'm going to miss that hair, those eyes, and this smart mouth."

He stopped in front of her, only inches separating them, and reached out to run his thumb along her bottom lip with one hand, slowly undoing the loose knot in her robe with the other. His pupils dilated, his breathing stuttered, and even in her lust-addled mind, she felt a smug satisfaction that her body, naked under the robe, could have such an effect on such a man.

She could see that he was fighting harder than usual to hang onto his control. To keep on the right side of that line he'd drawn between them.

But Francesca had already decided that they were crossing that line. Her body, her future, and her life were hers to do with whatever she wished. And in truth, there was never going to be anyone for her but him. So, if he didn't feel the same, if she were to remain a spinster because he didn't want her forever, then so be it.

She'd been resigned to a single life anyway. Had rather been looking forward to it, truth be told. So why shouldn't she have this? Men could do so and not have it ruin their lives, therefore, she could, too. And he would never tell. Not if she didn't want him to. Did that make her some sort of morally gray concubine? Perhaps. But she didn't particularly care. Not when she already knew the pleasure he could give her. And knew there was so much more yet to take from him.

"Most of all, I'm going to miss being free to do this," he whispered before cupping the back of her neck and pulling her forward for a savage kiss.

Francesca gave herself over fully to Adam's expertise. The feel of his clothing against her bare skin sent gooseflesh breaking out across her body. But she didn't want clothing separating them. She didn't want anything separating them tonight. She gripped the front of his lawn shirt and tugged it loose from his breeches before sliding her hands beneath the material to press against the hot, rigid hardness of his abdomen. He groaned into her mouth at the contact, the sound making her head spin.

Cheska pulled back, keeping her eyes locked on him as she slowly shrugged the satin robe from her shoulders and let it pool at her feet, exposing all of herself to his ravenous stare.

"You are perfect," he rasped.

"And you are too formally attired," she countered, but it came out shakier than she would have liked. Still, he smiled at her and without hesitation pulled his shirt over his head.

Francesca's mouth dried at the sight of him. He was beautiful. There really was no other word for it. Despite how muscled and masculine he was, how tall and broad shouldered, handsome just didn't do him justice. And she loved him with a fierceness that could easily overwhelm her.

He had given her so much of himself over these past few weeks. Had opened up to her, shown her the deepest, darkest parts of himself. He had made her laugh and smile and even cry. And he'd brought her to such exquisite heights of pleasure that she sometimes thought she might die under his touch. And still, she wanted more.

Wordlessly, she reached out and skimmed a hand down his torso, his heart hammering beneath her touch. He just stood there and let her touch her fill. She noticed a scar that she hadn't seen before, jagged and angry, just under his ribcage, and lifted inquiring eyes to him.

He held her stare, but some of that bleakness of old bled into it. "I ran afoul of an enemy sword," he said gruffly, and Cheska felt a surge of panic at the words, though the memory of it couldn't hurt him now. Not physically, at least. She bent and pressed a soft kiss against the skin, hearing him shudder above her.

And then she dropped to her knees in front of him.

"Francesca," he started to speak but cut himself off with a hiss as she boldly reached out and pressed a palm against the rigid length of him, stroking just once before moving to unbutton his breeches, hoping he wouldn't notice the trembling in her hands.

He'd shown her how to please him with her hands and had

told her of doing the same with her mouth, but she hadn't yet done it. And she wanted to. Tonight, she wanted everything. With shaking fingers, she undid the last clasp and pushed her hands inside the waistband, freeing him fully.

His hand reached down, tangling in her hair, the grip tight and edging on painful, but that only excited her more. She had no idea what she was doing but gave herself over to instinct as she leaned forward and took him into her mouth.

>>><<<

ADAM COULDN'T CONTAIN the black oath that hissed from his lips at the feel of Francesca's mouth around his cock, at the sight of those lips upon him, her hair falling around her shoulders. He could do nothing but hold on for dear life and let her guide this. As much as he wanted to take control, she was in charge. And he told himself that right up until her tongue flicked against the sensitive underside of the tip and his control snapped.

Fisting her hair, he gritted his teeth and prayed he wouldn't spill into her like an unseasoned lad, but damn, it was exquisite. And he could no more stop himself from taking control and guiding her head back and forth than he could stop the sun from rising.

He lasted only moments before the pressure began to build at the base of his spine, and he used the shredded vestiges of self-control to stop her movements and pull her to her feet.

"Did I do something wrong?" she asked wide-eyed, and a harsh laugh was torn from him. "Hell no, Sunshine," he groaned. "You did everything exactly right. But I want my turn."

He watched in fascination as a delicate blush painted her cheeks, marveling that she could do so when she'd just been on her knees for him.

But when he moved toward her, she put a hand up to stop him, her palm pressed against his heart. "What's wrong?" he asked, frowning.

"I have a request," she said, her tone oddly formal given that he was half naked and she was fully so. "And I want you to keep an open mind." He dragged his eyes down the length of her body, his mouth watering, his hands itching to touch.

"I am in no mood for negotiations, love," the endearment slipped out, but he didn't regret it. Not when it was stamped in the very soul of him. He'd wanted to tell her in any case. But not yet. Not until he heard news from the letter he'd sent. "Whatever you want, it's yours. Whatever you need, take it. Just don't tell me to wait."

Her smile was pure, feline seductiveness, and it nearly brought him to his knees. "In that case," she said, her voice steady and clear. "I want you. All of you. Everything."

It took a moment for the words to sink in, for Adam to be able to think around the blazing desire that roared through him when he understood what she was saying. He wanted to wait. They *had* to wait. He wouldn't have her thinking that when he offered for her, and he would, it was because she was somehow ruined. When she would never be anything but utterly perfect in his eyes.

He opened his mouth to tell her so, but there was that glint of determination in her eyes. That stubborn tilt of her chin. And the fact that she was still gloriously naked. No man could withstand that combination.

"I know what I want. I don't care about some arbitrary rule about how I should act, what I should feel, or who I should give myself to. My body and my–my heart," she stumbled slightly, and his own heart stuttered, "they are mine to give to whom I choose. And I choose you."

Him. Broken, jaded, damaged him. It was the greatest honor. The greatest gift.

"I'm not asking for anything beyond tonight, Adam."

He shook his head slightly, wondering how he could have been granted such a gift after everything he'd done.

"I was never going to let you go after tonight, Francesca," he said quietly, a little cockily. But no more. He would tell her no more, ask no more of her until he knew the outcome of that letter. Until he'd put that final ghost to rest.

Her brow lifted at his arrogant tone. Even now. But he didn't give her chance to deliver a setdown with that mouth of hers. Instead, he moved quickly as an asp and plunged his tongue inside her mouth, lifting her and wrapping her legs around his waist.

The feel of her core pressed against him was exquisite torture and it snapped something inside of him. Made him feral. Uninhibited. Adam tossed her on the bed, then stood back to remove the breeches she'd unbuttoned and watched with pure male satisfaction as her eyes widened and traveled down the length of him. Every scar, every ridge, every muscle was exposed to her now.

And when she smiled and beckoned him closer, he knew that she would always accept every part of him and find beauty even in the ugliness. He banked his desperation as much as he could, and his brow beaded with sweat as he fought to restrain himself as he kissed and licked his way down her body, as he brought her to release with his tongue and his fingers.

And when he finally positioned himself between her legs, and she reached up and ran a finger along the scar at his temple, he pushed inside and gloried in her cry of wonder.

"Adam," she gasped, her legs wrapping around his hips and pulling him closer, further into the agonizing, exquisite tightness of her. He gritted his teeth to stop from plunging deeper inside. "Please."

"I don't want to hurt you, love," he rasped, rocking his hips to let her get used to the size of him.

But he should have known that even this would be on her terms. She rolled her eyes, actually *rolled her eyes* in the middle of this most life-altering thing, and then lifted her hips and pulled him inside until he was fully seated.

His black oath filled the silent recesses of the room. He

couldn't help it. She felt perfect. More than he could have even imagined. But he'd caught her wince of pain, and he never wanted to hurt her. Never again.

    He pulled back slightly, meaning to tell her he'd stop. If that's what she needed, he'd find a way to stop. But his movements elicited a moan. Not of pain, but pleasure. And when he moved again, pushing further, creating a steady, rolling rhythm, she moaned again, his name on her lips. "Please," she whispered, "more." Her hips found his rhythm and matched it. And when she exploded beneath him with a cry, his release came, too, blurring his vision and turning his world entirely upside down.

Chapter Twenty

SOMETHING WAS WRONG. Even in her sleep, Francesca could tell. Slowly, too slowly, she came awake. She moved, her body twinging in places it never had before, and she smiled to herself, that sense of foreboding easing as the past few hours played out in her head.

Her night with Adam had been better than she ever could have hoped for. And every time she'd thought her need had been sated, or indeed his, he'd look at her a certain way, or kiss a certain spot, or even just sleepily reach for her, and it would rise again, quick as a flash.

He'd brought her to heights of pleasure she couldn't have imagined. And afterward, he'd taken such good care of her that she'd felt her throat tighten and her eyes fill with happy tears. Though, of course, she wouldn't let tears fall. She never cried if she could help it, and she certainly wasn't going to start blubbering all over him.

A groan sounded beside her, and she whipped around to face Adam. His face was contorted with pain, his body soaked and trembling. That's what had woken her. The man she loved was in the throes of one of those unspeakable nightmares.

"Stop," he gasped, his hands clutching the sheets. "Please. Not her."

She didn't know what to do. Panic licked along her veins, and her heartbeat skittered. She wanted to help, but if he lashed out, if she got close and he hurt her again, she knew he wouldn't come back from that. Yet to see him in pain, to hear the agony in his voice? It was unbearable.

"Francesca!" The scream tore from him, loud enough to wake the dead and frightening enough to set her into action.

She had no idea how she'd ended up in his nightmares, but she couldn't endure it. Couldn't just watch this happen to him. A flicker of fear made her ashamed of herself, but she ruthlessly pushed it back. Even if he hurt her, she assured herself, it wouldn't be on purpose. She could endure it.

"Adam," she spoke softly at first, not wanting to startle him. But it did nothing, and his dry, rasping sobs were like lances to her heart. "Adam," she called more firmly this time. More demanding. There was still nothing. Still only torment.

So, taking her courage in both hands and praying that he didn't lash out, for his own sake as much as for hers, Cheska leaned over him, grasping hold of his face and holding him still. "Adam," she practically shouted and knew that between them both they'd probably woken Sophia and half the servants. But she couldn't worry about that now. "Adam, I'm here. It's all right. I'm here. I'm here."

He took a deep, shuddering breath and time seemed to still before his eyes suddenly opened, and in the moonlight streaming through a gap in her curtains, she could see that they were wild. Lost to that panic that had taken hold of him during the thunderstorm. Before she knew it, he'd flipped them until she was pinned beneath him, the breath whooshing from her body.

Once again, fear tried to take hold, and she pushed it away. "Adam," she kept her tone soft, soothing, hoping that it might get through to him. "Adam, it's me. I'm here. You're safe." Still that wild, unseeing light in his eyes. And then she remembered what he'd been yelling. *Not her. Please not her.*

"*I'm* safe, Adam," she tried again. "I'm with you, and I'm safe." She reached unsteady fingers up and carefully pushed a lock of sandy hair from his brow. "I'm with you."

She held her breath, her heart thudding painfully. Then slowly, his eyes cleared, and he blinked down at her, his jaw clenched. "Francesca." The rawness in his tone almost killed her, but she kept her eyes firmly on his. Letting him see that she was fine.

"Did–did I hurt you?" he gasped.

"No," she responded immediately and with absolute conviction. "You didn't. I promise."

He studied her for an age, but finally, his shoulders sagged with relief as he saw the truth in her eyes.

"Do you want to tell me about it?" she asked softly as he pushed himself off her and lay back against the pillow. He pinched the bridge of his nose before turning his head to face her.

"It was the usual sort of thing except…" He shuddered, the remnants of his terror darkening his green eyes. "Except you were there. And you were surrounded, and I couldn't get to you."

"Why do you think you dreamt of that?"

His lips quirked in a crooked, heart-rending smile. "Because I don't want you to leave. Because I'm afraid to let you go. Afraid to lose you."

Her heart stopped. And she didn't know how or even if she should have this conversation. To confess to him what was in her heart. "You're not losing me, Adam," she whispered. "I'm coming back tomorrow to organize my party."

A soft laugh escaped him. "*Your* party?"

"It might as well be," she said with faux severity. "I'm the one doing all the work."

He laughed harder at that, and she was glad to see his breathing was easier.

"Perhaps I don't want you to leave at all," he said, his smile fading. "Ever."

Her poor heart was suffering terribly with all the stopping and starting it was doing, and she opened her mouth, not quite sure what to say in response. But he reached over and pressed a finger to her lips.

"There is so much I want to say. So much that needs to be

said. But not now. Sleep, Sunshine. And when the time is right, we shall have that talk, you and I." He leaned over and caught her lips in an exquisitely tender kiss. But before that ever-burning passion could consume them again, he slipped from the bed and quickly threw on his clothing. Then with only a glance back at her, and a quick, tender smile, he was gone.

A WEEK LATER, Adam sat in his study brooding. He was supposed to be going over the household accounts and the various reports from his estate stewards. Making plans for the spring and beyond. But inevitably, his mind was on Francesca.

The house felt so bleak without her that he'd taken to sneaking into her bedchamber, where her scent still lingered, remembering every detail of that night together. He saw her almost every day since she was in the throes of organizing *her* party. His lips twitched at that. But she had been correct. It *was* hers. Everything he did now was with her in mind.

Yet, still, he missed her. He missed just knowing she was near. Solitary meals and lonely nights were an agony now that he had lived the alternative. Hell, he even missed Sophia, who'd returned with Francesca every day under the guise of helping. He'd yet to see her lift a finger, however. In fact, he'd only ever seen her trying to sneak off with his horse.

The problem was that it was getting harder and harder to find any time alone with Francesca. Her family had thrown themselves into helping with the festival with concerning enthusiasm, though he suspected her brothers-in-law only did so to stay close and watchful.

And because there were so bloody many of them, he'd taken to following her around like a pathetic puppy begging for scraps of attention. He hadn't even had the chance to kiss her since their last night together. What had become of him, sniffing around her and pining after her when she wasn't there? And why didn't he particularly care if it meant he was close to her? Because he was smitten. Absolutely and irreversibly.

A knock sounded on the door of his study, and he leapt up hoping it was Cheska, even though it was far too early, even for her. But it was only a servant bringing the post. He nodded his thanks as he reached out to grasp the correspondence, flipping idly through letters from his solicitors in London, his man of business in Spain, and a letter from an old friend. A Scottish duke who, despite Adam's best efforts, had never truly left him alone.

He'd called on him in London, the letter said, and been informed of his stay here. *I know you'll refuse,* the letter went on to say, *but I'll be near Halton before Christmastide on my way home for the yuletide. Let me know if you might allow an old friend to check on you and make sure you are well. And I have news to share in any case, Heywood. News that you might need to see to believe. Write to me at my home in Mayfair. Yours etc, The Duke of Farnshire.*

Adam's lips twitched as he read over the missive. Devon Blake was nothing if not irreverent, and he knew the duke didn't expect an invitation to visit or even a response. But he thought of Christmastide. Of the winters he'd spent here with his father and Douglas. Of a Christmas day with Francesca and her family, happy and laughing and watching the children play, some of whom he'd met when they'd come along with the Templeworth ladies and run riot around his house and staff.

Perhaps having a friend to visit wouldn't be so bad. And a part of him, a smugly male part, wanted to show Francesca off. To let his old friend see that he *was* well. Better than well. He was happy. Or at least he would be when he finally proposed to the woman he loved. For he did love her. Every single thing about her. And he wanted to shout it from the rooftops.

He tossed the letter onto his desk, vaguely wondering about what Farnshire would have to show him, when the last letter in the pile caught his eye and his heart stopped.

He hadn't been expecting to hear back from the investigator

so soon. When he'd sat and written that letter, giving the man all the information he could remember about Davy and what he'd been told about Molly, he'd thought it would months to track something down. But here was a letter from Mr. Bowler.

He dropped the letter onto the desk and moved to pour himself a measure of brandy, tossing it back straight away. He replaced the tumbler carefully, afraid that he might shatter it, before steeling himself and turning back to the letter.

So much hinged on the content of that missive. In a way, his whole future. Because this was something that he knew he had to set to rest. If he were to be the man Francesca needed, and the man she deserved, then he needed to be whole, or at least on his way to it.

He sat on the chair that had been his father's before him, staring at the letter as though it might bite him. Either way, he had to know. And so, he reached out and opened it.

Chapter Twenty-One

"I REALLY DON'T think the constant entourage I arrive with is necessary," Cheska groused and was promptly ignored by said entourage. Although to be fair, it was only her sisters today, at least. Usually Gideon, Christian, and the children came along, too.

Just yesterday, she'd watched, her heart melting, as Adam had crawled around the lawn at the front of the house chasing after George and Ollie with Lily and Ella on his back, hitting him with sticks and screaming at him to go faster.

He'd looked up at her at one point, his eyes a bright emerald in the Autumn sun, and smiled with such tenderness, that she nearly threw her nieces off him so she could drag him away for some privacy. Unfortunately, her overprotective brothers-in-law were no better than watchdogs and would have noticed her slipping away to have her way with the marquess.

"We're just excited about the festival," Hope said, too innocently to be sincere.

"Yes, and it is a huge undertaking. You need the assistance," Elodie added.

"Honestly? I'm just here for the horse."

"Yes, thank you, Sophia. That was helpful," Hope drawled.

"At least she's *being* honest," Cheska pointed out.

There was a moment of silence whilst the sisters walked arm in arm up the path to Heywood Manor. And Francesca idly wondered when she'd started to think of the place as home.

"Fine, we want to be here when the marquess proposes. Happy now?"

Cheska drew to a stop so suddenly that she ended up dragging them all backward. "Wh-what?" she stuttered.

Her sisters just grinned at her. "We're not blind, Cheska. That man is so besotted with you it's a wonder he doesn't melt into a puddle at your feet."

"Indeed, he's almost as nauseating as you are."

"You should have heard the noises coming from the pair of them before we returned home."

Sophia's casual announcement brought about a stunned silence, and Francesca felt her cheeks heat under their scrutiny. But she raised her chin and refused to look away. She felt no shame for her actions. She loved Adam, and even if she didn't, she'd had a marvelous time.

"Don't look at me like that," she warned her older sisters. "I do not believe for one moment that Christian and Gideon acted in any way appropriately with either of you." Elodie's blush and Hope's grin were all the answers she needed to that particular accusation. So, she turned her ire on Sophia. "And what were you doing listening to that?"

"I didn't have much of a choice in the matter, Francesca. I would rather have listened to Nell squall for days. *Believe me.*" That was fair enough, Cheska supposed.

Sometimes she found it hard to stomach being around Elodie and Christian, or Hope and Gideon. Or at least she had. Now, she would be more than happy to join their ranks and just spend all her time making Sophia feel sick until she, too, found a man to make her swoon.

Never would she have imagined herself the swooning type, but there it was. Adam had ruined her completely, and in more ways than one. For while he'd been worried about her reputation as a respectable lady, she'd been worried about seeming like a simpering idiot to her sisters. But clearly, they were on to her, and she saw no point in denying it.

"So, do you think he'll propose before the festival or on the night of it?" Hope asked excitedly. "Elodie thinks he'll wait because it's more romantic, and he knows how much you love it. But I think it could be at any moment because frankly, he looks at you like he wants to eat you alive, and I'm not sure how much longer he'll hold out."

"He didn't hold out," Sophia snorted.

"I…" Francesca didn't know what to say. How to explain the complicated situation with Adam. "We have no understanding. He's made no promises, and I have asked for none." The silence that her statement was met with felt so awkward that for the first time in her life, Francesca didn't want to look her sisters in the eyes.

"But–but you've …" Elodie started to speak, then trailed off, sharing a speaking look with Hope and Sophia.

"Yes, I have. He has. We have." Cheska answered the unspoken question. "And I don't regret it because I love him. And it's not as though I were saving myself for a husband, is it? You know I've never had an interest in marriage, in being owned by a man who sees me as nothing more than a broodmare. So, who was I supposed to be saving myself for?"

Her outburst was met with yet more silence, and for some bizarre reason, Cheska felt like crying.

"Quite right," Sophia said with a nod, but the other two merely watched her.

Eventually, Hope broke the silence. "Well, was it any good?" she asked, and Cheska couldn't help laughing at Elodie's gasp of shock.

"Extremely," she answered with no small amount of smugness.

And then her sisters wouldn't rest until they heard details, even Elodie. When she'd finished, Hope was making a show of fanning her face. "Take note, Sophia," she said. "Choose wisely as your sisters have and find a man who knows his way around a bedchamber. And around a—"

"I think she gets the idea," Elodie interrupted before Hope could say anything too vulgar. She turned a serious gaze on Cheska then. "But if he asked you, not because he sees marriage as ownership but because he loves you as Christian loves me, as Gideon loves Hope, would you accept?"

"It's complicated. With Adam. He…" Cheska paused, not quite knowing how to explain without telling her sisters about his struggles. And she would never want to break his confidence. To share his story. "He went through some things that were very difficult for him," she said, settling on the easiest explanation of something that she didn't quite understand herself. "During the war and afterward. After old Lord Heywood died, and his brother died in battle he's just, perhaps he's not ready to take that step."

It wasn't much of an excuse, but it would have to do, for Francesca had no idea if Adam would *ever* want to marry and have a family. Or if she'd be the one he'd want that with. She thought so. With the way he held her and kissed her and looked at her as though she were the moon and the stars to him, she sometimes thought he must be in love. And he'd said more than once that he didn't want to let her go. But he'd never said the words, and she wouldn't demand them of him when he was healing from so much.

"Poppycock," Sophia scoffed. "I don't care how complicated it is. That man loves you, and you love him. When it comes down to it, I don't think anything is insurmountable when you have that. And you should know better than to doubt that, Francesca Templeworth. You are usually the clever one."

Francesca could only gape at her younger sister, who never seemed to pay much attention to any living being that could talk back to her. Yet, here she stood, sounding wise behind her years and filling Cheska's heart with hope.

"I suppose we shall just have to wait and see," Francesca said, trying and probably failing to keep her tone light and nonchalant. Inside, she was quaking, and she suddenly couldn't wait to see

Adam again. To look into his eyes and see if she could find evidence of what her sisters saw.

"Are we taking bets then? On when he does it?"

"That would be unseemly, Hope."

"Oh, hush, Elle. Who cares? I'm all for Francesca finding happiness and all that tosh, but if there's a bit of coin to be made out of it, so much the better!"

"Fine. Ten guineas say he waits until the festival."

"I say he'll do it just before. So that he can announce it and watch to see if Mama faints clean away when she finds out she can add the title of marquess to her sons-in-law."

"As soon as he gets her alone. That's what I think."

Three sets of eyes turned on Francesca, who rolled her eyes but couldn't help the burst of elation. She should tell them she wouldn't involve herself in a wager about her own life, but she didn't really have a choice since she was usually the one who took care of their bets anyway.

"I think he'll wait a while," she said, finally giving in and allowing herself to get caught up in the infectious excitement of her sisters.

She didn't tell them why she thought he'd wait. That he might need to sort through some of his more difficult feelings before proposing. After all, he hadn't told her that he loved her. But her sisters were convinced that he did, and so maybe he was just biding his time. Maybe he *was* planning a romantic surprise at the festival.

Despite her best efforts not to get ahead of herself, Cheska couldn't stem the butterflies of excitement she felt as she hurried up the path, eager to see Adam. She knocked on the large, oak door and waited impatiently for a footman to open it, her sisters whispering and giggling behind her.

The door was soon opened, and she was admitted straight away. By now the staff all knew her and knew that she was planning the festival in any case. Footsteps sounded on the marble tile, and she spun around hoping to see Adam grinning at her in that way that made her toes curl. But it wasn't Adam. It was the butler, Hodges, who had been invaluable to her these past few days.

She smiled at the old servant, surprised when he remained grim-faced. "Hodges, is everything well?" she asked. He hesitated. Something she'd never seen him do. And Francesca felt a sudden sense of dread. "Could you please tell Lord Heywood that my sisters and I have arrived?" she continued, wondering why he hadn't immediately led her to the drawing room and offered refreshments. That's what he'd been doing every day since she'd moved back home.

"Ah, Miss Templeworth, h-his lordship is not at home, I'm afraid." The butler looked as though he wished the ground would open and swallow him whole.

"Oh, that's fine," she said airily, though she couldn't shake the feeling that something was amiss. "We shall head out to the gardens to see about where to set the stalls. If you'd like to join us, we can make a plan to show Lord Heywood when he's back."

"I'm afraid that the marquess isn't coming back, Miss Templeworth," the butler said softly, and Cheska's body froze in shock. "At least not in time for the festival."

"What? Don't be ridiculous, of course he's coming back," she scoffed. But her laugh sounded brittle even to her own ears. Behind her, her sisters fell quiet.

"He bade me give you this, Miss Templeworth," the butler held out a letter. And yes, that was Adam's handwriting. The festival was supposed to be happening tomorrow night. How could he just have left? How could he not even see her? Where could he have gone? She simply stared at the letter, not moving to take it when a hand reached over her shoulder and took it from the servant.

"A tray of tea in the drawing room please, Hodges." The voice was Elodie's, dear, sweet Elodie who would never usually invite herself to tea in someone else's house when he wasn't even there. "My sister has had a bit of a shock, you understand."

"Of course, Lady Brentford," the old servant said, sounding relieved to have something to do and rushing off to do Elodie's bidding.

"Come along, dear," she said softly, taking Cheska's arm and pulling her toward the drawing room. "Let's get to the bottom of what's going on here."

Francesca allowed herself to be pulled into the drawing room, hardly knowing what to feel or say or think. He'd left her. Just like that. After—she swallowed a lump in her throat—after she'd given herself to him completely and utterly. What if he'd just been using her and now…

"Whatever it is you're thinking right now, don't," Sophia said stoutly, pushing Francesca into a damask armchair. "Just read the letter. I'm sure there's a good explanation."

Francesca dutifully took the paper, hands shaking so much she didn't even know if she'd be able to read it. She ran a thumb over the Heywood seal embedded in the wax before breaking it open and reading. Her sisters remained a quiet, steady presence by her side as her eyes skimmed the paper and saw what he'd written. As her brain took in every word, every detail.

And when she jumped to her feet, every one of them screeched in fright. "I have to go," she said urgently, turning and dashing from the room, vaguely aware that they ran right after her.

Chapter Twenty-Two

"He only left this morning, there's still time to catch him."

"Yes, we understand that part, Francesca. We just don't understand *why* we're catching him."

"Has he absconded with a floozy?"

"How is that helpful?"

"I just think it best to consider all possibilities."

"What on earth is going on in here?"

The four sisters turned to see Christian standing in the doorway of Francesca's bedchamber, glowering at them all. "Nothing," they said as one, and his face paled dramatically.

"Oh hell," he said. "What have you done now?"

Francesca didn't have time to feel affronted. She let her sisters explain what was going on while she finished stuffing money into her reticule and grabbed the riding jacket Sophia had lent her.

"What?" Christian's explosive question likely meant that Elodie had finished her hasty explanation. "You are absolutely not leaving this house to travel alone. On a horse. In *breeches*. To a village at least a day's ride away."

Francesca merely raised a brow at him.

"I mean it," he said. "I seriously mean it. You cannot, I will not..." He drew to a close as the four sisters stared at him. "Fine," he huffed out. "Wait for me to ready the carriage. It shouldn't take too long. Then I will *escort* you to this village of yours, and we will find Heywood together. That seems reasonable, does it not?" She heard the desperation in his tone, so she nodded.

"It does," she said, and he breathed a sigh of relief before dropping a kiss on Elodie's head and hurrying from the room, probably so she couldn't call after him and change her mind. But she wasn't going to change her mind. And it *did* seem reasonable. Except that she'd already made up her mind to go on horseback, and his idea's reasonableness had little to do with it.

As soon as Christian was out of earshot, Elodie turned back to her. "So, are you ready to go then?"

Cheska blinked in surprise. "You're not going to try to make me wait for Christian?"

"Absolutely not. I know you can't tell us what is so urgent, but I know it's important to you. And since you once helped me stowaway in Christian's carriage, it's only fair I return the favor and help you get away now." Cheska pulled Elodie into a brief but fierce hug.

"Come on, it's clear to go."

It was so similar to a few years ago when they were helping Elodie to escape an unwanted marriage to the pig farmer that Francesca felt a bit nostalgic as they all tip-toed down the staircase and out the door to the stables.

"He's on Ares, so there's no way you'll catch him," Sophia said as they skidded to a halt in the stable. She set about saddling one of her own horses, a beast so big and feisty that Francesca felt a flicker of fear as she eyed it.

"I might," she answered, pulling her eyes from the giant horse. "I must try. He needs me."

She knew her sisters were curious, but they wouldn't ask for anything more than the sparse information she'd already given them. That Adam had something in his past that haunted him. That he'd left to finally lay it to rest. And that he didn't want to burden her with it, so he'd gone alone. Her heart had broken for him to know what he was going to do.

She reached inside the pocket of the riding coat and ran her eyes over the letter again whilst Sophia finished saddling Monty, and Hope and Elodie argued by the entrance of the stable about how to distract Christian and Gideon, should they arrive.

"I still think a bit of nudity is the quickest and by far the easiest way to do it," Hope was saying.

"Yes, but there are servants everywhere, Hope."

Cheska just shook her head and tuned back to her letter.

My dearest Francesca,

I don't have time to go into all the details that I wish to share with you. I received word from an investigator that I hired to search for Davy's family and perhaps, if I were very lucky, his Molly, too. I told you once that his family lived a day's ride from Halton or thereabouts.

He found them.

I know you'll understand when I tell you that though I dread facing them, I feel ready to put this part of my past that I've been holding onto for so long to rest.

I'm beyond sorry to leave you like this. I want nothing more than to stay by your side, always. But if I ever want to be worthy of that honor, then I have to face this part of me. Face it and begin to move on from it. Only then can I truly tell you what is in my heart and what I wish for, with every fiber of my being.

I'm sorry to miss your party, Sunshine. But I hope to be able to throw you a party every day for the rest of your life if that is what you desire.

Yours. Always.
Adam.

"Right, if you manage to stay on top of him, Monty will get you there in one piece."

Sophia's voice sounded as Cheska finished the letter, and she hastily stuffed it back into her pocket, sending a prayer of thanks heavenward that neither of her older sisters had as yet felt it necessary to start disrobing in the middle of the stable.

Sophia put two hands on her shoulders and stared into her eyes, the blue of hers almost an exact replica of Francesca's. "You have always been the bold one, Cheska," Sophia said softly. "Always courageous. Always confident. I suspect that Adam will need that now. Need you." She hugged Cheska to her right as Hope cursed loudly enough to wake the dead.

"He's on to us, Cheska," she yelled, and Sophia quickly grabbed the step to help Cheska into the saddle.

"Run," she said. "I've already hidden Christian's saddle, but it won't take him long to find it."

"Good luck, dearest," Elodie called.

Cheska kicked Monty into a trot, then a canter, and made for the field that would take her onto the road out of the village. And as she dashed off, she could just hear Hope's voice floating on the wind toward her. "Elle, I think it might be time to take off your dress."

>>><<<

ADAM SAT IN the corner of the small but clean inn, nursing a tankard of ale and wishing he could be anywhere but here. He knew it was edging toward too late to call on Mrs. Hubert's home. Especially with what he had to say. But he just couldn't do it. Not yet. Not now. He missed Francesca. He hadn't realized how much he'd come to rely on just being around her to help keep the monsters at bay.

But this wasn't something he'd wanted to drag her into. He wanted her to laugh with her sisters, play with her nieces and nephews, dance, and drink cider at her Autumn festival.

Some part of him knew that doing this, letting go of Davy and the suffering he'd held onto for all these years was the right thing to do. And he was ready to do it. Ready for the ghosts of his past to rest in peace. Ready to live with the woman he loved and appreciate every blessed day with her.

It was just hard to take that step.

"Hubert!"

A cry went up across the taproom, and Adam's head snapped up, his shoulders stiffening, his eyes darting around to see who the person was calling to. There at the entrance stood a man who could have been Davy had he survived the war. Adam could only watch, locked in memories as the man raised a hand to the friend that had called out to him and began moving toward him.

He couldn't take his eyes from this Hubert fellow. His smile, his loud, bellowing laugh. Is that what Davy would have been like if he'd been given the chance to grow older? To live in this small community with friends and family nearby?

Adam's heart beat faster and faster. He couldn't drag his attention from the man across the room. And the longer he looked at him, the more he sank into those memories of Davy talking so lovingly about his family. About his love. His desperate, futile dash through the field that had been like a hell realm. His body lying too still, his eyes too glassy. And his hands clasped around that curl…

A crash from a nearby table jolted through Adam, and suddenly he was back there. The crash was a gunshot and not a clumsy serving wench with a trayful of ale. The raucous laughter became the cries of the damned. Killers and those they killed. The room warmed by cozy fires became a cesspit of death and destruction. And he was trapped in the middle of it.

This isn't real, he told himself desperately, trying to cling to that truth. But it was fading, moving further and further from his grip. He had to get out. Out from his own head and out of this inn. He had to remember something real. Something to hold on to and help him to focus on why he'd wanted to do this, why he'd needed to.

His heart thundered, and every shout reverberated through him, dragging him back into the hellhole of his memories. He had to get out. He had to try to remember something good. Something in this new life that he'd decided to fight for. To live for.

Francesca.

The idea of her was just strong enough to give him the wherewithal to stand from the table. Somewhere in the back of his mind, he knew that he was causing a commotion as he jumped from his stool, sending it tumbling to the ground, knocking over the table and its contents. He was vaguely aware that the music and laughter and chatter had stopped as he staggered toward the door, his stomach churning, his heart hammering.

He couldn't seem to catch his breath, couldn't get enough air into his lungs. He needed to get *out*.

Adam burst through the door of the inn, gulping down breaths of the crisp, evening air. Why did he think he could do this? He couldn't. There was no escaping the darkness of his memories, his mind, his soul. He never should have come here, and he never should have thought that there was a way back from this for him. Staggering into the courtyard, surprisingly empty for this time of the evening, he bent over to lean on his knees and try to breathe. If he could just breathe, then maybe he could find his way back to the light.

With the noise of the inn behind him, the waking nightmare started to ease at least. He wasn't back there on that field of death. He was home. He was safe. He was free. But he knew, coward that he was, he couldn't face Davy's family and tell them that he'd watched that poor boy die. And maybe that meant he wasn't worthy of Francesca, and he would lose the only good thing he'd ever had. But maybe he didn't deserve that type of happiness anyway.

The sound of galloping hooves caught his attention, and Adam looked up, desperate for any sort of distraction from his maudlin thoughts. One rider. Small and slight and oddly familiar.

He stood straighter now and watched, that familiarity tugging at the frayed edges of his mind. He knew that body. That mass of golden hair. It couldn't be. But it was. He looked on, stunned and confused and so damned grateful that he nearly sank to his knees.

She'd come. Impossible though it seemed, dangerous as it inevitably was, that was Francesca in breeches and riding astride, headed straight for him. And he could do nothing but let a tear fall as she came.

Chapter Twenty-Three

ADAM CLOSED THE distance between them until he was reaching up and pulling Francesca from the horse, staring into her eyes with a mixture of elation, sorrow, that haunting panic and, she thought a little nervously, definitely some anger directed at her.

"Please don't tell me you came here alone," he growled by way of greeting. Not "thank God you're here" or "I've missed you since that one night we had together" or "now that we have a moment, I'd like to confess my undying love to you." Just a clipped question that wasn't really a question at all.

"Do you see anyone else with me?" she asked snippily and realized that for all her worry, she was angry at him, too.

But before she could deliver any sort of answer, he suddenly pulled her against his chest and squeezed the life out of her, burying his face in the top of her head. "I thought you were angry with me," she gasped, though the sound was muffled from being pressed so tightly against him. Not that she was complaining.

"I'm furious with you." He pulled back enough to glare down at her. "Do you have any idea what could have happened to you, being out on these roads completely alone? The danger you could have found yourself in? I don't know whether to kiss you or wring your neck."

She scowled up at him and prepared for a fight of epic proportions. She was tired and hungry and had spent *hours* worrying about him, about what manner of awful thing awaited him. Yet here he was, scolding her as though she were nothing more than a disobedient child.

But as he stared at her, she saw it. Beneath the ire was real, gut-wrenching fear. Fear for her. After everything they'd been through these past weeks, and the way he'd opened up to her, she'd come to see them as something of a team. Yet at the first opportunity, he'd left her.

"I wouldn't have had to be alone if you hadn't left me behind," she said. "You shouldn't have left me like that," she continued, unable to keep the hurt from her tone, though she tried. "I would have helped. I *want* to help."

His eyes flashed with some intense emotion. "I'm sorry," he said, the picture of contrition. "I didn't want you around this," he continued, but the words were broken, and when she reached up to place a hand against his heart, she found that it was still beating frantically. "I haven't even called on his family. I've been sitting here like a damned coward and then…"

"What happened?" she encouraged gently when he trailed off.

"I couldn't go there. Face them like that. I thought I could, I wanted to, but I couldn't. And then a man came in who looked exactly like him."

She reached up and cupped his face with her hand, uncaring that they might be seen by any number of people.

"You don't have to do this now," she told him firmly. "If you're not ready, we can just go home and talk about it. I can help you. Let me help."

He was already shaking his head, and she tried not to feel rejected.

"I didn't want this for you," he whispered. "I wanted to be whole again. Not drag you into the mess inside me." He took a shuddering breath. "I just wanted to protect you."

Francesca took a step away from him and crossed her arms. She didn't feel that usual flair of irritation when a gentleman talked about protectiveness, as though females were utterly helpless without them. Because she knew that Adam didn't think that way. But it still rankled, and *if* they were going to be together, she needed to be very clear about something.

"No. That's not how it works, I'm afraid. Not with me. You don't get to protect me and coddle me and act as though I'm some helpless *thing* for you to cosset and fuss at. If you care for me, then you must treat me as an equal. And if you get to protect me, then I get to protect you, too. Even if it's from yourself. And this is never something you should have tried to do alone. Something you should *have* to do alone."

He just stared at her, so she plowed on.

"You are the most courageous man I know. You fought for your country and witnessed unspeakable horrors, yet, still, you've tried to continue your father's legacy. But being brave doesn't mean facing everything by yourself. Sometimes the bravest thing to do is lean on somebody else. So lean on me, Adam. Because I don't want to be protected from you. I don't want some perfect version of you that you've decided I deserve. If I cannot have you exactly how you are, then I don't want you."

She didn't know how he'd take what she said. There was every chance that he'd be a typical, boorish male and insist that he could do everything alone. And she wasn't quite sure what she'd do if that were the case. Slap him, probably. But he merely stared at her for an age, his eyes bleak, his skin pale.

And then he pulled her into his arms once again. Not to kiss her, just to hold her, perhaps to steal some of that strength she spoke of. And she heard his whisper even as his lips pressed against her head. "Thank you."

ADAM MADE LIGHT work of procuring a room for Francesca. He still had that shaky, hollow feeling inside of him, but taking care of her had at least given him something to focus on. Although, he thought with a wry smile, if she found out he was taking care of her, she'd probably have his head.

He kept his eyes deliberately away from that table in the corner while he inquired after a bath and a tray to be brought up to the room. Ordinarily, he would have stayed down here so that she could see to her ablutions in peace, but he couldn't face sitting there and seeing the man that could have been Davy, so he'd just wait in the corridor until she was done.

He hadn't missed the gleam of speculation in the innkeeper's eyes when he'd asked about a room. A single room. And he knew that he should have gotten two, but frankly, he needed to be near her. Not only to know she was safe, for his heart still pounded in fear at what she had done, at what could have befallen her, but for himself, too. Because she was right—he needed her. More than she could possibly imagine.

And miracle of miracles, she wanted him just as he was. So, when the lecherous old innkeeper had boldly asked who the young lady was, Adam hadn't hesitated in saying that she was his wife. His marchioness. He hoped to make it so soon in any case, so what harm was there in saying it now? At the very least, it might stop speculation and rumor spreading about her. Not that she'd care about such things. He smiled wider at that, imagining what she'd have to say to anyone who called her behavior into question.

The innkeeper's wife, a far more pleasant individual, came bustling out to inform him that hot water was being readied and that a tray would be provided momentarily, and he nodded his thanks before hurrying back up the stairs, ignoring the particular bark of laughter he could hear above all others in that taproom.

Tomorrow. He would deal with it tomorrow. And he would have Francesca right by his side whilst he did so. The comfort that thought alone brought him was breathtaking.

He knocked on the door of their room and entered, his throat closing at the sight of her standing by the fire.

He hadn't had the chance to look her over properly when

he'd been in the throes of panic. But he could do so now. Lazily and thoroughly. So, he let his eyes drift from the hair she'd unbound from the braid down to the loose white shirt that billowed around her, the jacket already disposed of on the chair, and the skintight breeches that made his heart damn near stop. She was glorious. And for the first time since that night they'd shared, he had her alone with no chance of an interfering family member popping up from somewhere.

She raised a brow at him as though she could guess at the direction of his thoughts, and indeed, there was that blush that he so loved bringing to her face. Prowling toward her, he let his mind drift from the struggle that awaited him tomorrow. Tonight was about her. Just her. And he planned to enjoy every second of it.

He reached out and grabbed hold of the front of her shirt, pulling her toward him, and filling his smile with everything he meant to do to her. But just as he dipped his head, a knock sounded on the door and a curse of frustration tumbled from his lips. He felt her breathless laughter against his lips as she moved away from him to the door.

A servant stood with a tray of food, and Francesca quickly directed her to the small table by the window. When they were alone again, she turned to smile at him. "I hope you're hungry," she said, waving a hand at the veritable feast on the table.

But he kept his eyes only on her. "I'm ravenous."

Chapter Twenty-Four

FRANCESCA LAID HER head against the edge of the tub and sighed in bliss as the rose-scented water eased the ache of hours in the saddle. She had no idea why Sophia enjoyed it so much. From here on in, she would be traveling on foot or in a carriage. Though she'd have no choice but to get back on the horse tomorrow after they met with Davy's family.

She felt a little flutter of anxious anticipation when she thought about it, so she could only imagine what Adam was feeling. And that was exactly why she'd insisted on hurrying after him. She heard movement in the hallway and rolled her eyes.

He'd insisted on waiting outside to give her privacy, even though she had no problem with him seeing her in the bathtub. She had no idea why he'd insisted on it in any case. Knowing him as she did, she'd read that hunger in his eyes and knew what he had planned for them. Demanding that he sit on a rickety old chair in the corridor was foolish in the extreme.

An imp of mischief awoke in her, and she smiled to herself. He needed to loosen up. He'd told her to call out when she was ready. She was ready now.

"Adam," she called, then laughed at the distinctive sound of a chair hitting the ground. He was inside before she'd even finished calling his name, and came to a complete standstill, his eyes blazing as he ran them over her still lying in the tub.

She ran her own gaze over him, noting the bulge straining

against his breeches that turned her core to pure, molten heat. This need for him, would it ever go? She didn't think so.

Swallowing a lump in her throat, she boldly held his stare. "You told me to tell you when I'm ready," she said, her voice slightly hoarse at the blatant desire in his eyes. He didn't speak, just nodded slowly. "Well, I'm ready."

Her words seemed to be a red rag to a bull, and he darted forward to pull her from the tub, water sloshing everywhere, soaking him in the process. He'd freed himself of his jacket while they'd eaten, and in seconds, his shirt was completely transparent, clinging to every muscle and making her mouth water. It had been too long, far too long since she'd been with him like this. She let every bit of her frustration and need for him show in her kiss. His mouth was savage upon hers as though he too couldn't control himself. And she didn't want him to control this lust for her. She wanted every raw, overwhelming piece of him.

His growls were animalistic and drove her wild, and when he lifted her from her feet, it was pure instinct to wrap her legs around his waist. He turned her, not to the bed but to the nearest wall, and she gasped into his mouth at the feel of the cool stone against her heated skin. She tore at his sodden shirt so she could slip her hands beneath it, so she could grab hold of the buttons of his breeches.

Maybe they should slow down, she thought, but she'd missed him, missed *this* so much. And if she had her way, there would be plenty of time to go slowly on other occasions.

Finally, the buttons gave, and she was able to release him, relishing in his groan as her hand stroked against him, guiding him to her entrance. She hadn't known that making love like this was possible, but she acted on instinct, being led by what her body was craving.

Adam suddenly hefted her higher, pulling his mouth from her body and staring right into her soul as he pulled her hips down in one, powerful thrust. She cried out at the sensation of being so full, thinking she would die from the pleasure of the feel of him buried inside of her. Thinking it couldn't possibly feel better, until he began to move.

He controlled her movements, using her hips to guide her body down onto him over and over in a wild joining. That knot of torturous pleasure grew tighter and tighter until suddenly she exploded, her cries of pleasure melding with his own.

She was panting, struggling to get air back into her lungs, but when he leaned forward to kiss her, she didn't hesitate. Keeping her upright with one arm around her waist, he reached out and pushed a sodden lock of hair from her forehead.

"You're exquisite," he gasped, wonder and awe in his eyes.

She smiled with pure feminine delight. "You're not too bad yourself, soldier," she grinned, earning herself a bark of laughter.

"I'm glad to hear it," he quipped as he walked them to the bed. She groaned as she stretched out, her muscles screaming in protest. "I need to rest my aching muscles," she complained as he stripped off the rest of his clothes and slipped between the sheets, pulling her closer and holding her tight.

"Keep making those sounds, and you'll be getting no rest, love. Believe me." And despite the fierce coupling they'd just had, her body broke out in gooseflesh at the sinful promise in those words.

"Sleep," he said, running soft kisses along her neck and shoulder. "Rest. You're going to need it."

She laughed softly, but he continued to kiss her and smooth a hand along her arm, and soon, she felt herself drifting into blissful sleep.

→»»×«««

ADAM LAY AWAKE watching the sun rise through the window of their room. Beside him, Francesca slept peacefully, her hair spilling across the pillow. She looked like an angel. But he knew the heat, the passion that lurked beneath the surface of that doll-like exterior.

Despite the mind-shattering encounter they'd shared when she'd called him into the room while she lay there with nothing on her except a seductive smile, he wanted more. He was insatiable when it came to her.

He was dreading this morning when he'd finally face Davy's family and hopefully find out what happened to Molly, but even that wasn't enough to dampen his lust for the woman asleep beside him. It was, however, enough to give him the strength to slip from the bed and the temptation she presented and hurriedly throw his clothes on so he could go belowstairs and find some food for her.

He felt a twinge of guilt that she was missing her own party that evening. And it was too late to stop it now given that the entire village of Halton had been invited and accepted. But he couldn't deny that he was glad she was here. More than glad. He knew he was only going to be able to face this with her beside him. He'd make it up to her, he vowed to himself.

The inn was quiet at this hour of the morning with only a few early travelers sitting and breaking their fast, so it was easy to get the proprietor's attention. After he'd requested a tray, Adam was able to inquire after the gentleman he'd seen last night. And the lady of the house, who seemed the type to know everyone, immediately confirmed that it had been Francis Hubert, the older brother of Davy and a gentleman farmer with property on the outskirts of town.

Adam returned to their bedchamber and slipped inside, trying not to wake Francesca until it was necessary, given how little sleep she'd had and how long she'd spent on the road yesterday. He still felt a pit of fear in his stomach when he thought of the many things that could have happened to her, but she was here with him now, safe and unharmed, and he would make sure she stayed that way.

Not trusting himself to get back into the bed with her, he sat by the window watching the world wake up as the courtyard below filled with coaches and horses and people going about their days. And when the knock came just a few minutes later signaling the arrival of their breakfast, he took the tray at the door, making sure to block the servant's view of Francesca.

He turned, tray in hand, to see that she was awake and sitting up, the sheets pulled up to cover her, her hair tumbling down around her.

"Oh good, I'm starved," she said by way of a good morning and jumped from the bed, uncaring of her nakedness, for which he was eternally grateful.

He set the tray on the table, and by the time he'd held out a chair for her, she'd donned his lawn shirt from last night, dry now because of the fire he'd kept blazing in deference to the cool weather. It was huge on her, falling below her knees, and he couldn't believe the sense of satisfaction he got from seeing her in his clothing.

As they ate, she told him about how today would go to prepare for the festival, and he felt guilty all over again. But when he tried to apologize, she simply reached out to him and grabbed his hand. "There is nowhere else I would want to be," she told him, her eyes filled with sincerity. And if he hadn't already loved her to distraction, he would have fallen in love right then and there. In turn, he told her what the innkeeper's wife had said, and when she asked if he was ready, he found that he was. At least as much as he could be.

After that, it was only a matter of moments for them both to be dressed, with Francesca wondering if they'd be put off by her appearance, and Adam telling her he didn't care if they were. It was idle chatter to keep the reality of the situation at bay, he knew. But before long, there was no more reason to delay, so he took a deep breath and led them to the stables, keeping hold of her hand the entire way.

Chapter Twenty-Five

"THIS IS IT."

It was the first time Adam had spoken since they'd left the courtyard of the inn. Cheska hadn't wanted to engage him in meaningless conversation unless he started it, knowing that he was struggling.

Her muscles were in agony from a day in the saddle and then the night she'd spent with Adam, but she wouldn't say a word about her discomfort. She would just remain by his side, there if he needed her. It was early, too early for calls, really. But since the family were farmers and kept country hours, they'd guessed that they would be able to receive them. And she knew, too, that Adam just wanted to get it over with now that the time had finally come.

She looked at the well-situated farmhouse that had appeared as they crested a hill. In the low morning sun, the windows sparkled, and the sounds of livestock and laughter floated through the air. All around them were fields with bales of hay and wildflowers. It looked a beautiful, peaceful place. She didn't know why she'd expected it to be gloomy.

"Are you ready?" she asked him softly, turning in time to see his grimace.

"Not really," he said with a small, sad smile, and she wished she could protect him from this or somehow do it for him. But he needed to do it himself. "But I'm glad you're here," he added.

They made their way toward the house, Francesca's heart hammering so loudly she was surprised he didn't comment on it. She watched him closely for signs of distress. His breathing grew shorter, and his skin paled the closer they got.

They drew to a stop at the front of the house, and Adam dismounted before turning to lift her from Monty. He stared into her eyes, his hands tightening at her waist, and she saw the flicker of terror in his gaze. There was no way to help him do this, no way to make it better, so she only reached up and took his face in her hands.

Now wasn't the right time to tell him what was in her heart. To tell him that she loved him with every inch of herself. But that was exactly how she felt, and as soon as this was done, in whatever way it ended, she would be telling him. Because even if he didn't feel the same, he deserved to know that he was not unlovable or unloved.

"I'm right here," she said instead. "I won't leave your side." And that would have to be enough, for just then, the door to the farmhouse opened, and on the step stood not a woman old enough to have borne a son Davy's age but a much younger woman, with chocolate-brown curls.

ADAM STARTED AS the woman appeared. There were plenty of women in England with brown, curly hair he told himself. This could just be a coincidence. It might not be Molly, whose curl he carried even now in his pocket.

The woman was pretty and plump, an apron tied over her dimity gown, a babe only a few months older than Nell by the looks of it, perched on her hip.

She looked at them curiously, but her face was open and her smile friendly.

"Can I help you?" she asked as Francesca pulled him toward

her, and she looked between the two of them with wide, hazel eyes.

Hadn't Davy said Molly's eyes were hazel?

Francesca turned to Adam, waiting for him to speak, but he found himself rendered utterly mute. He knew he was staring like a dolt, but he couldn't help it.

"Er, hello," Cheska stepped forward again, pulling him with her. "We were looking for Mrs. Hubert."

"I am Mrs. Hubert," the woman answered.

"Oh, um, we were actually looking for an older Mrs. Hubert," Cheska said politely.

"Ah, my mother-in-law," the smiling woman said. "I am Molly Hubert, her son Francis's wife."

Adam felt his entire body freeze at the casual statement, and he felt even Francesca stiffen by his side.

"You—" Francesca was floundering, turning confused, pleading eyes to him, and it was that look, the look that said she needed him, that snapped him out of that state of frozen shock and into action.

"Mrs. Hubert," he pushed past the dryness in his throat. "You do not know us, but I am Adam Fairchild, Marquess of Heywood, and this is my—" He stumbled to a close, having no idea how to describe Francesca. "This is Francesca Templeworth," he continued, feeling her eyes on him. "—I fought in the war alongside—"

"Davy?" Molly's whisper was filled with fondness and heartache, and it was all Adam could do not to cry himself as a lone tear ran down her face. "You were Davy's officer-in-command."

"I was," he said hoarsely. "And I was with him. On the battlefield. The day he died I was—I tried so hard to…"

Francesca reached out and squeezed his hand, giving him the strength to continue. "I was with him when he died. He fought bravely until the end."

Molly just stood and listened, tears tracking silently down her face, the baby in her arms cooing and babbling, having no idea of the horrors being discussed around her.

"I should have come sooner," he continued brokenly. "I should have found you and his family as soon as I was recovered. I should have told you that he was a wonderful soldier and a better man. And that he loved you, all of you, fiercely."

He let go of Francesca's hand and reached into the pocket of his riding coat, wordlessly holding out the parchment.

She hefted the child a bit so that she could open it, and when she did, the broken sob that fell from her lips was a sound Adam would take to his grave. But as she fingered the curl that he'd kept all these years, the reminder of that brave lad and so many like him who'd fallen and been left behind, she looked up at him with eyes not filled with reproach and disgust as he'd expected, but with love and gratitude. And kindness.

→»»—«««←

FRANCESCA SAT SILENTLY and sipped her tea with shaking hands. She felt a little foolish for crying, but then everyone was crying, so at least she didn't stand out. The Huberts' drawing room was clean and cozy and roomy enough that she, Adam, Molly, her husband Francis, and Mrs. Hubert, Davy's mama, fit comfortably inside.

After that initial introduction, there had been a flurry of activity with Molly urging them both inside, then sending the maid to fetch Mrs. Hubert and track down Francis. While they'd waited, she'd explained how she'd stayed close with Davy's family, helping them through their grief while they helped her through hers.

And over time, she said, as they all learned to live around this hole in their lives that would never be filled, affection for Francis had turned to love. A different kind of love. A love borne of companionship and sharing something so awful and turning it into something good.

Mrs. Hubert had arrived next and listened to Adam's tale before she'd taken him into her arms and hugged him, a mother's hug and one that Francesca saw he'd needed, his knuckles white as he gripped the kind woman's shawl.

And finally, Francis came accompanied by a young boy, a boy named Davy for the uncle he would never meet, and Adam was able to tell them all about their Davy and how brave he'd been, how pure and kind and good, even in the face of so much that wasn't.

She'd managed to keep little Davy and the baby called Anne occupied so that Molly could talk with Adam, and she offered up a silent prayer of thanks that she'd been blessed with nieces and nephews so she knew what to do with them.

When the maid had come to take the children for a nap, she'd taken her seat beside Adam. His shoulders were drooping slightly, and she knew that he was exhausted in the way that one became when something took a huge emotional toll. But he seemed happy, too. No, not happy. But a little more at peace with himself than he had been. And after a while, he looked at her and declared that they should take their leave.

There was another flurry of goodbyes, hugs, and kisses, and promises to write until finally, they were outside and alone.

She dared not question him as they readied their horses, trying to give him a moment to process everything that had happened in the past two hours. But as soon as the stable lad had left them, Adam turned to her and pulled her round to face him. She looked at him, unsure of what to expect. But then he smiled, and her heart caught. For it was a smile she hadn't yet seen from him, a smile so like the one he used to wear before the world had stolen so much of his joy, that she found herself beaming up at him in response.

And when he kissed her, she threw her arms around him and kissed him back with every fiber of her being, with every ounce of love she felt for him, and every hope for a future contained within her heart.

She could practically feel the tension leave his shoulders as he held her, and when he pulled back and took her face in his hands, just as she had done to him only hours ago, his eyes held a look of peace that they hadn't before. There would be a long road to travel for him, she knew. But this was a start. A wonderful, healing start.

"Let's go home," he said softly, and she nodded before he lifted her into the saddle.

Nothing had ever sounded so wonderful to her.

Chapter Twenty-Six

ADAM LASTED FOR about two hours of seeing Francesca wincing in the saddle as they started their long, arduous journey home before he decided he couldn't allow her to make the entire trip like that. He wanted her to make it to her party, he really did. But not if it meant her being uncomfortable or in pain.

His head felt strangely clear now. After such a harrowing and emotionally draining morning, he'd expected to feel worse. But no, while he couldn't say that he was anywhere near recovered from the war, he could say with certainty that a little piece of his heart had healed in that homely drawing room on that small, unassuming farm.

He hadn't realized how much he'd needed Davy's family to forgive him until they'd offered him not censure but understanding. Not anger but gratitude for being a friend to their boy. And to see that Molly had managed to find some happiness in this world was a balm to his damaged soul.

And he would have none of that tentative peace, know none of that quiet joy were it not for the woman by his side. So perhaps she would be late to her party, but he couldn't in good conscience allow her to suffer.

They came upon an inn, and he insisted that they stop. After escorting her to a small but serviceable private dining room and ordering her some tea and cakes, he set about finding them a carriage. There weren't many options available to him since this wasn't exactly a bustling town like London or Liverpool, but he managed to get them a conveyance that while not exactly luxurious was clean and certainly better than horseback.

He paid far over the odds for a gig, and knew that if his friend Devon Blake, who was an avid lover of horses, or Sophia whose love bordered on obsession, were to see him attach such a vehicle to Ares and Monty, he'd never live it down. But he had no choice since the owner of the gig wasn't willing to part with the horses that pulled the damn thing.

And he didn't care how foolish it looked or how crazy it might be, he would do anything to save Cheska from any type of pain. He would never be able to repay her for the strength and support she'd given him today. For helping to navigate him through that meeting with Davy's family. And for sitting by his side, silent and steady, as he spoke of the lad who he hoped now was resting in peace.

Nor would he ever forget that joy he'd felt, a joy so intense that it stole his breath, when he'd seen her play with the children, scampering around with the little boy and cuddling and singing softly to the babe.

He could see it then, laid out before him in his mind, Cheska's belly round with his child, that love and unyielding strength passed down to boys and girls, whose hair would shine like sunshine and whose mischievousness would keep him constantly on his toes. And he wanted all that. So badly that it hurt.

Maybe this time alone was the perfect opportunity to tell her that.

He couldn't help but laugh when he took her back outside and presented the gig to her, when her squeal of delight and shout of "oh, thank goodness," echoed around the courtyard. And when he sat her in the gig and she moaned in pleasure, bouncing up and down on the cushion and declaring that she would never set her backside on a horse again for as long as she lived.

It was a ridiculously tight fit with their saddles having to be tied onto the conveyance with a rope that he prayed would hold, but she was so thrilled anyone would think he'd gotten her a royal carriage made of solid gold.

They fell into a companionable silence, broken every now and then when they pointed something out to each other, or when he asked her to regale with him outrageous stories of her pursuits with her sisters. They were a bunch of absolute hellions, Adam concluded after a particularly uproarious tale of a gentleman in London whose hands had become far too wandering, and the sisters had ended up convincing him to strip and take a dip in a fountain in Vauxhall Gardens, then stolen his clothes and run home, leaving him to find his own way completely naked.

Of course, the plan had been Cheska's idea, though it had been Hope who'd gotten him to strip, Sophia who'd tricked his driver into leaving his carriage so she could drive it home, and Elodie who'd kept watch because she knew she couldn't stop them. But she could, hopefully, stop them from being thrown into Newgate.

At least, he thought to himself, if all went well and Cheska agreed to be his, he could help Brentford and Claremont to look out for Sophia, who was the wildest of the lot and would likely need them all watching her like a hawk.

The day wore on, and as they stopped for luncheon and then dinner, as they rested the horses and the afternoon bled into the evening and then night, Adam thought of what to say to her. Which words he could possibly use to convey just how deeply he loved her. How she'd pulled him back from a life of only darkness and despair. And how he wanted to marry her so that he could spend every day of his life trying to give her even a fraction of the happiness she'd given to him.

He turned his head slightly to finally tell her what was in his heart and saw that she'd fallen asleep. The bitter tang of disappointment coated his tongue as he realized he'd missed his opportunity. He'd have to wait now until he got her alone again, and damned if he knew when that would be. Especially because he had a feeling that when Brentford and Claremont got their hands on her, she'd be locked in a tower somewhere after the stunt she'd pulled in coming after him.

So, swallowing his disappointment, he turned the gig and headed to his manor, burying the words that he so wanted to shout from the rooftops.

⇒⇒⇒⇐⇐⇐

"THERE YOU ARE! I knew you wouldn't miss it. I told you, Hope."

"Well, forgive me for thinking she'd take the opportunity to enjoy her time on the run with a dashing marquess."

"What in God's name have you done to those horses? I'm going to murder you."

Francesca awoke suddenly to a cacophony of shouts and saw that they'd arrived not just in Halton, but at Heywood Manor, and she was being accosted by her sisters. They climbed into the gig to drag her down, and she allowed herself to be pulled, still half asleep and wondering what was going on.

"Mama has been looking for you since yesterday," Elodie said. "But we managed to convince her that she'd just missed you every time she asked. And when you *do* see her act as though you're sick. But not too sick. Just sick enough to have missed your meals."

"Yes, and when you see Christian and Gideon, run."

"Come on, I brought a gown with me in case you made it back, even though I hoped you wouldn't. Honestly, Cheska. I expected better from you. Or worse, I suppose, if you catch my meaning."

"Damn it, Gideon's spotted you. Seriously, run. And Lord Heywood, I think it might be an idea for you to run, too. I'm almost positive I saw Gideon bring his pistols."

Francesca's head was spinning with the information being thrown at her, and she looked over her shoulder at Adam as her sisters dragged her away. He was staring at her with something like regret in his eyes, but before she could insist on going back to him, Gideon appeared and smacked a none-too-gentle hand onto his shoulder.

She didn't hear their exchange, but she could guess at it being not entirely pleasant as Adam grimaced but nodded once, and then both gentlemen turned to walk in the opposite direction to the one in which she was being pulled.

Her stomach was churning with anxiety as her sisters pulled her toward the bedchamber she'd occupied whilst staying here. It felt like a lifetime ago, yet everything was just as it had been, the bed freshly made up as though the staff had expected her to return.

"I sent for hot water the moment I saw it was you arriving," Elodie said. "There won't be time for a bath, but you should be able to wash and make yourself decent."

"That's fine," she answered automatically. "I had a bath last night."

There was a moment of stunned silence before Hope smiled wickedly. "So, we won't be able to make you decent then," she snorted. "It's not magic water."

Cheska reached out to flick Hope's arm, then squealed when she returned the favor.

"Are you going to tell us what happened then?"

A maid arrived with the water Elodie had requested, and Cheska quickly washed her face and hands while Sophia began brushing her tangled hair. Hope hurried out to collect the deep gold gown she'd selected to be worn under Cheska's navy-blue, crushed velvet cloak.

Once they were all assembled again and pinning up her hair, waving away the maid so they could talk in private, Cheska decided to tell them everything. Or as much as she could without breaking any of Adam's confidences.

"Wait," Sophia suddenly shouted as they all made their way back downstairs and to the festival. "The party is already on. I've lost the bloody bet. It's not fair. It's not my fault they ran away."

And the sisters laughed and squabbled and debated the terms of the bet all the way down to the festival below.

Chapter Twenty-Seven

ADAM SAT IN awkward silence waiting for the interrogation that he expected and even accepted, albeit grudgingly. He had to remind himself that he was glad that Francesca had people that cared about what happened to her. Especially since by all accounts, Mr. Templeworth cared not a whit what happened to his daughters, even before he'd grown ill.

He sat behind his desk, nursing his brandy, and trying not to pull at his cravat under the scrutiny of the two men staring daggers at him. And it did indeed look as though Claremont carried a pistol.

"You know that we cannot just allow you to traipse off to God knows where with Francesca?" Brentford began, and Adam sat back, thinking of what to say. It galled him to sit here feeling as though he were back at Eton being scolded by his tutors. But on the other hand, Francesca was a single lady, and they were entitled to know that she wasn't being used ill.

And yet...

"Forgive me, Brentford. But didn't you spend weeks alone on the road with your wife *before* she was your wife?"

The viscount blinked at the question before his mouth twitched, and he nodded at the hit. "Touche," he said. "But as you say, she is now my wife. And I knew very early on that I would marry her. That, I think, makes all the difference."

Beside him, Claremont snorted, and Brentford turned to glare at him. "What?" he asked hotly.

"Oh, nothing," the earl shrugged. "I just wondered if Elodie knew you would marry her or if you had kept that little tidbit to yourself while you were seducing her around inns all over England."

It was Brentford's turn to snort then. "And am I to believe that you kept your hands to yourself around Hope until after you said 'I do'?" he asked.

"That was different," Claremont answered. "I loved her from the moment I saw her. So—"

"So, you get away with it? I don't think so."

Adam listened to the two lords bicker back and forth and realized that their situations weren't all that different. None of them, it seemed, could come away from an encounter with a Templeworth unscathed.

"Regardless of which of us was the biggest blackguard," Brentford said when they'd reached something of an impasse, "the point is that we love our wives and that means we love their sisters, too, and we consider it a duty and a privilege to be able to look out for them."

"Quite right," Claremont chimed in. "And that means that we can't and won't allow anyone to hurt Francesca or Sophia."

They turned their attention back to Adam, and he could only shrug.

"Francesca deserves to hear what I have to say before anyone else," he began. But when he saw their eyes narrow simultaneously, he decided to throw them something of a bone. "What I can say, gentlemen, is that you should understand me perfectly when I say that we have all suffered the same affliction. And it is my dearest wish that I will soon be in a position to watch out for the sisters, too."

There were a few seconds of tense silence before Claremont and Brentford relaxed, shaking his hand and clapping him on the back, and insisting that they drink more of his expensive brandy before rejoining the party.

And Adam heard from behind him as he dutifully moved to refill their glasses, "I told you that you wouldn't need the pistols."

"We'll see," came the ominous reply. "She hasn't said yes yet. And if I know anything about Francesca, it's that we should never assume what she will or won't do."

THE FESTIVAL WAS a roaring success. Especially considering it had been thrown together rather last minute. Everywhere Francesca looked, people were smiling and happy. There was music and dancing and, there in the middle, a bonfire that looked big enough to touch the sky.

She talked to everyone who came to speak to her. Dutifully oohed and ahhed as her nieces and nephews showed her the horse chestnuts and pinecones they'd found. And she listened to her mother braying at the neighbors about how taken Adam was with her. She wished that her mother wouldn't say such things, especially because Adam would hate to be the subject of their gossip.

As soon as she had the opportunity to slip away from her mother, she took it, gratefully accepting a mug of the apple cider she loved so much and wandering away from the crowd to stand alone under a large oak tree at the edge of the celebrations. She wished that she wasn't so exhausted, wished that she had the energy to dance around with her sisters and their husbands, who'd just appeared to sweep their wives into their arms. But the last two days had taken their toll, and she found herself wondering if she'd be caught should she slip away to her old bedchamber.

"I suppose I shouldn't be surprised that you managed to pull off quite a spectacular event with only weeks in which to do so."

Cheska turned at the sound of Adam's voice behind her. The light from the bonfire flickered over his face, casting it in light and shadow, making his eyes a startling green.

She shrugged nonchalantly. "My sisters helped."

"Yes, but I distinctly remember hearing your voice barking orders like an army general," he said in all seriousness. "If my footmen hadn't all been half in love with you, I think they would have quit on the spot."

She rolled her eyes, taking a sip of her cider. "Well then, maybe you need footmen made of sterner stuff," she responded, earning herself a chuckle.

A silence fell between them, filled with a tension that Cheska couldn't name but which set a riot of butterflies fluttering in her stomach.

"Do you want to dance?" he asked softly, his voice deep and almost guttural.

"I would love to dance with you," she answered honestly. "But I'm afraid that my body might give out completely if I do. I am *not* built for days of traveling on horseback, even if some of it was, mercifully, in that gig you acquired."

He laughed again but soon sobered, reaching out to stroke his knuckles along her cheek. "I know I've said it already but, thank you. For yesterday and today, yes. But for so much more, too." Francesca's heart stuttered at the earnest words. "I'm not sure I'll ever fully be able to convey just how much it meant to me, and just how much you saved me, Sunshine. But I will try. Every chance I get, I'll try. If you let me."

Maybe he didn't mean what she thought, she tried to reason with herself. Maybe he just meant that he'd keep up a correspondence or something when he moved on to one of his other properties. Potential meaning after potential meaning flitted through her head until she'd convinced herself he was going to run off and never see her again.

But the hand that had brushed her cheek moved to tilt her chin up.

"Look at that busy mind at work," he quipped. "And it doesn't look as though it's thinking anything good."

Francesca took a deep breath, wondering what to say and then deciding that she'd always been honest to a fault and perhaps she should just continue that tradition right now.

"I'm wondering what exactly you mean by every chance. After all, you have no fixed plans as far as I'm aware. For all I know, you could mean that you'll pay a polite call on me every time you're in Halton or something."

"Is that what you really think?" he asked, amusement dancing in his eyes.

"Not really, no."

"So, what do you really think?" he coaxed.

Time for more of that honesty, she decided. "Frankly, I'd rather not say," she blurted. "Because though I'm not often wrong, it has been known to happen in the past, and I'm quite terrified of this being one of those rare occurrences, so I'd rather just stay quiet and let you explain yourself."

A stunned silence met her little outburst before he threw back his head and laughed; the sound lighter and more carefree than any she'd ever heard from him. When he finished, he reached out and took her mug from her, tossing it and its contents into the grass at his feet.

"I was drinking that," she complained hotly, but soon quietened as he reached out and took both her hands in his.

"I will never have a dull moment with you in my life, Francesca Templeworth. And I must confess that makes me so excited, I cannot wait to begin." She knew some of her impatience was showing on her face when he grinned at her in a way that said he knew he was annoying her. But truly, though it was lovely to be standing here chatting, if he had something important to say, she wished he'd just get on with it, so she could tell him she loved him and hopefully convince him to join her in that plan to slip away to her bedroom.

Yet, as soon as his expression grew serious, all impatience and wantonness flew from her head until there was only him and the moonlight and her bonfire that reached the sky.

"I am broken and damaged," he began softly. "But not beyond repair. I know that now because you have fixed so much of me just by being in my life. And I know that if I have you by my side, I will be able to walk the path to being a better man. I will be able to fight my demons and come back to the light."

Francesca felt her eyes fill with tears. He had come so far, and he was right, she would walk through the fires of hell for him if that was what he needed.

"But broken and damaged as I am, I love you. I love you with every scarred piece of my heart. With every fractured part of my soul. And I will love you every moment of every day for as long as I live in this world and for an eternity in the next. You are everything to me. My light. My salvation. My sunshine."

His words set off an explosion of pure joy inside Francesca's chest, and she threw her arms around him, her tears flowing freely now. But she let them come. She didn't care that he would see her cry. She would let him see every part of her because she knew that he would love every part of her, just as she loved every part of him.

Adam held her close for a moment before pulling back slightly so he could look into her face. "I want to marry you," he said softly. "And I do have fixed plans. I plan to be wherever you want to be, for however long you want it. I plan to dedicate my life to being worthy of you and making you happy. If you'll have me," he tacked on wryly.

She smiled up at him through her tears, hardly daring to believe this was real. Hardly believing what a romantic sop he was turning her into.

"Of course, I'll have you," she sniffled. "If only because Mama will positively die to have a marquess for a son-in-law."

Once again, his laughter rang out through the night air. And he leaned down to kiss her, but she stopped him with a hand to his chest, feeling his heart beating at the same frantic rhythm as her own.

"I love you," she said softly, sincerely. "I love every broken, scarred part of you. Your darkness and your light. You are the best man I've ever known, and you make me happier than I ever thought possible. I only ever want to be where you are, for however long you are there."

And this time when he bent toward her, she let him kiss her, their love now declared and out in the open, turning the kiss into something so tender, so passionate that she was worried they'd set fire to the trees around them.

And as she and Adam were besieged by her sisters and their husbands *and* their children, she distinctly heard one voice ring out over the noise. "You all owe me ten guineas."

Chapter Twenty-Eight

"Do YOU REMEMBER this place?"

Cheska turned to smile at her fiancé, delighting in the fact that she could call him that. With the wedding only weeks away, her mother had gone into a fit of organizing. Cheska largely ignored it all. She didn't care what she wore or what they ate or who was there to witness it. All she cared about was that she would belong to Adam, and he would belong to her, and they would get to be together forever.

He came up behind her and wrapped his hands around her waist, pulling her back against his chest and pressing a kiss to her neck. Ever since they'd announced their betrothal, he'd been like a man possessed, trying to get her alone at every opportunity. Not that he had to try very hard since she was more than happy to be alone with him. And Sophia had been invaluable since she was always on hand with her particular brand of chaperoning. Namely going off on a ride on Ares and leaving Cheska and Adam alone for hours.

He looked at the river just ahead of them, the trees bordering it a study in reds and golds and browns. "Should I?" he asked.

Sometimes his memory wasn't entirely up to snuff, especially when his head ached from his injury or after he'd had a nightmare, though he promised her they were growing less frequent.

She smiled and shook her head. "Not particularly," she answered. "It probably didn't mean anything to you." She turned in his arms and wrapped her own around his neck. The weather was growing colder by the day, and her red velvet redingote was doing little to stave off the cold. "But when I was sixteen, right before you went away, you came here to fish, and I followed you. I had a bit of an infatuation with you, you see."

"Did you now," he asked with a cocky grin.

"Yes, I did. Not that you would have noticed or cared. Anyway, I asked if you thought that your path would lead you back here, and you said one day."

He frowned in confusion at her, and she silently took his hand and led him toward a weeping willow that hung over the river. Pushing aside the branches, she stepped under them, pulling him after her toward the trunk.

She dropped onto her haunches, uncaring about the muck getting on her ivory skirts, and he dropped down beside her. "Look," she said, pointing to a carving in the trunk. She felt him go entirely still beside her as he saw his name carved into the tree, surrounded by a heart.

"I've never told a single person I'd done this," she confessed softly. "I never would have lived it down if my sisters had found out. But, after you'd left, I thought about your path leading you back here. And I thought that maybe, if it didn't, then there'd be a part of you here always. When the news came that you were presumed dead, I came here every day for weeks just looking at it and hoping that if you hadn't managed to find your way here, you had at least found your way to somewhere peaceful."

She turned to look at him and saw unshed tears gleaming in his eyes.

"I know you forgot us," she said. "And that you forgot this place. But I never forgot you, Adam. I kept you with me from the day I carved your name here."

She would have said more, but his lips pressed against hers, and he whispered his love for her repeatedly against her mouth. And later, when he'd shown her just how much he appreciated what she'd done, and she sat in his lap so that she wouldn't completely ruin her skirts, he kissed the top of her head and smiled at her.

"I finally found my way back to you," he said. "My home."

Chapter Twenty-Nine

"This has become a spectacle," Francesca groused as she stood outside the packed church in Halton.

She had told her mother very clearly that she wanted a small wedding, yet Kit had informed her that the entirety of Halton was here along with the Hubert family and Adam's friend, the Duke of Farnshire. Actually, it was Devon's fault, she thought grumpily. Because when Mama had found out that a duke was attending, she'd turned into a frenzied madwoman, and now Cheska had to walk down the aisle with every single eye in Halton on her. It was unbearable.

"Just focus on Adam, dearest," Elodie said.

"Just try to imagine everyone in their undergarments," Sophia added, which was a lot less helpful and really quite disgusting.

"Just imagine *Adam* in his undergarments," Hope said with a wink, and that actually worked quite well.

In less than an hour, she'd be the Marchioness of Heywood, but more importantly, she'd be Adam's wife. The title she could learn to live with; the husband was the real prize for her. She let Elodie fuss at her veil and Hope fuss at the train of her satin ivory skirts whilst Sophia pushed a simple posy of roses into her hand. She'd had them tied with a yellow ribbon. Yellow for sunshine and for Adam's special name for her.

It had been a long, sometimes arduous road to get here, but

they were here, and she couldn't wait to get this part over with so she could be alone with her husband. A shiver of anticipation ran down her spine at the thought of it. They were going to sail to Spain for their honeymoon since Adam wanted to share that part of his past with her. She just wanted to be alone with him for as long as possible.

And when they returned, they were going to travel to his main seat, Heywood Abbey, so that she could start learning about her role as marchioness. At least in that respect, Elle and Hope could help her learn what it was to be the wife of a powerful peer.

Adam assured her that she'd do marvelously well but only because everyone would be afraid of her. She hadn't spoken to him for hours after that, but secretly she thought it had been worth it for the way they'd made up.

The doors to the church opened, and Cheska took a deep breath before raising her head, her eyes searching for Adam. And there he was, resplendent in his wedding attire and looking handsome enough to take her breath away. She kept her eyes trained on his as she stepped toward him and right toward her future.

IF HE LIVED to be a hundred, Adam didn't think he'd ever find a way to be as happy as he was today, dancing with his wife in his arms. When the doors to that church had opened, it had taken all his strength not to drop to his knees in front of her. He would never understand what he'd done to deserve calling this woman his wife, but he would spend his life working to be worthy of the honor.

"What are you thinking?" Her soft voice floated up to him, and he grinned down at her.

"I'm wondering how to get you out of here unnoticed," he said with a wink. It wasn't even a lie, not entirely. He'd been counting down the seconds until they could get away.

To his surprise and unending delight, she met his wink with one of her own. "Have you forgotten already husband that my sisters and I are quite the experts when it comes to escaping?"

He was momentarily distracted by the thrill of pleasure that coursed through his veins upon hearing her say that word. *Husband.* But then the rest of what she'd said sank in and he raised a questioning brow at her.

"What do you mean?" he asked curiously.

She merely looked down at his waistcoat. "Do you have your fob on you?" she asked.

"Of course," he answered swiftly, a sense of anticipation growing inside him.

"And what time do you have?"

He quickly took out the gold piece and checked it. "Just seconds until eleven," he said and was intrigued by her smile.

"Very well," she answered. "Get ready to run."

"Run?" he repeated. "What..."

A huge crash rent the air followed by more than one scream. But before Adam could even turn his head to see what the commotion was, Cheska had grabbed his hand and began dashing for the door that led from the formal dining hall and into the corridor beyond, straight out to the conservatory at the back of the house.

He was shocked to see Hope standing there grinning from ear to ear and holding a basket out toward him. "Here you go," she said brightly. "Enjoy yourselves. Gideon and I had a marvelous time on our honeymoon. Why on the first night he..."

"I'm not sure they need the details, my love," Gideon's voice came from outside where he held two valises, one in each hand. "Christian has the trunks already packed into the carriage. And you should hurry because Elodie said Sophia is a terrible actress and can't act as though she's fainted forever."

Adam reached out and took the valises, his mouth agape as Cheska pressed a kiss to Hope's cheek, then Gideon's, before

Gideon wrapped his wife in his arms and kissed her as though they were the newlyweds. Perhaps talk of their honeymoon had jogged a memory that Adam was quite sure he didn't want to witness.

He could only follow as Cheska darted around the side of the house. And sure enough, there was Christian standing by a carriage, a driver already in place. "Hurry up," he called jovially. "I'm not getting caught in the act by my mother-in-law." He kissed Cheska briefly on the cheek before handing her into the carriage, then turned to Adam, slapping him on the back.

"Welcome to the madhouse, Adam," he said with a grin as Adam climbed in beside Francesca. "I hope you're prepared for it." He shut the door with a thump, then ran off toward the house and disappeared inside.

Adam sat back, stunned by what had just happened.

But as his wife wasted no time climbing into his lap, he couldn't contain his smile of pure, unadulterated joy. Being around this incredible woman and her madcap family did indeed sometimes feel like a madhouse. But he was more than prepared for it. As long as he had his own personal ray of sunshine, he was prepared for anything.

About the Author

Nadine Millard is an international best-selling author hailing from Dublin, Ireland.

Having studied and then worked in law for a number of years, Nadine began to live her dream of writing when she had the first of her three children.

She released her debut novel in 2014 and has been writing ever since.

When she's not writing she can be found reading anything she can get her hands on, ferrying her three children to school and clubs, spoiling her cat, her dog, and snatching time with her long-suffering husband!

You can find out all about Nadine and her books at www.nadinemillard.com.

Printed by BoD in Norderstedt, Germany